Escapes
and Other Stories

CALUMET EDITIONS

Minneapolis

FIRST EDITION AUGUST 2025
Escapes and Other Stories. Copyright © 2025 by
Susan Bernadette Koefod. All rights reserved.

10 9 8 7 6 5 4 3 2 1
ISBN: 978-1-962834-37-7

Cover and interior design: Gary Lindberg

Praise for
Escape and Other Stories

"*Escapes and Other Stories* is an anthology to carry wherever you go and read in those moments when you need a lift or a laugh or a fright or a little drama to relieve the humdrum. It's really good!"

–David Housewright, Edgar Award-winning
author of *Them Bones*

"Susan Koefod's new book of short stories, *Escapes and Other Stories,* is an engaging and compelling collection that spans genres from the mysterious to the mystical to the meditative. Koefod has shown herself to be a talented writer who can bring her characters to life on the page and make you ponder. *Escapes* is the kind of book that invites you to brew a cup of tea, sit down, and enjoy."

–Allen Eskins, Barry, Rosebud, and Silver Falchion
Award-winning author of *The Life We Bury*
and nine other best-selling novels.

Escapes
and Other Stories

Susan Koefod

**CALUMET
EDITIONS**
Minneapolis

Table of Contents

Also by Susan Koefod

Albert Park: a Memoir in Lies

<u>Arvo Thorson Series</u>

Washed Up
Broken Down
Burnt Out

<u>Young Adult</u>

Naming the Stars

Iced

Henry Shaw blew into town every January with the bitter north wind. The moment he arrived, we knew it was over for the rest of us, even though his winning Winter Carnival ice sculpture never varied from year to year. His was the Mona Lisa to our best efforts—our glistening birds, shimmering creatures, and fantastical machines simply could not compete with his genius work. No one knew better the agony of losing to him than me. I finished second to him every year.

I might have had a chance of winning the year he wound up dead—his skull split by his own chisel and his beautiful ice sculpture dashed to bits—except that I was instantly considered the prime suspect in his murder.

Of course I resented his genius. I'm no angel. His death surely would have cleared the way for me to win the contest at last. But of all the competitors, I was the closest Shaw had to a friend. In the final hours before his death, I learned what haunted him to sculpt the same woman again and again. I alone knew the identity of his killer but feared that what I saw the night he was killed would do little to convince the authorities of my innocence.

* * *

Shaw achieved his artistry using worn, old-fashioned carving tools, leaving us to wonder what he might have gained by the advanced technology available—laser-guided chain saws and 3D computer models—not that any of us wanted to point out the merits of upgrading to him. He wasn't slowed at all by his humble gear. He chipped and shaped the thick block of ice rapidly, working with a steady urgency as if he were a heart surgeon trying to save a dying patient. He talked to no one and worked around the clock.

I always made a special effort to be friendly with Shaw. I felt it my duty to show good sportsmanship to the other carvers and Shaw himself. But Shaw seemed deaf to my courteous greetings.

"Why do you even bother?" Jess Laux, a young French-Canadian up-and-coming sculptor, asked me the day before Shaw was killed. I was, as usual, buying two cups of coffee and a couple of toasted bagels from a food truck vendor.

"What are you hoping to gain by brown nosing the guy? Trying to exploit a weak spot? Learn his secrets?"

"Just trying to be a good sport," I said, tossing a couple of sugar and creamer packets in my pockets before balancing a bagel on each of the coffee cups' plastic lids.

"I wish the guy would disappear," Jess said. "I'm tired of him winning every year. Aren't you about ready to kill him?"

"Now, now…" I said to the young guy. "Never let competition affect your actions or character."

He muttered a French-Canadian epithet and stomped away. With that, I picked up the cups and noticed that the coffee was so hot the cups warmed my hands through my thick buckskin choppers.

I carried breakfast to Shaw, and as usual, he seemed only vaguely aware that I had dropped by. His look was distant, his mind clearly on the work he was sculpting.

I couldn't help but whistle in appreciation of the beauty that was emerging from the ice. I knew, having closely observed him in the past, that it was the same woman once again. Yet she was even more beautiful than she had been the year before. Her serene face held a wide-set pair of ice-blue eyes. Her long, wavy hair flew in frozen swirls around her face, tousled by an unearthly breeze. She wore an almost transparent gown of silky ice of a vintage style that made her appear both timeless yet part of the distant past.

She was frozen in time and ice.

If it were possible, that year she seemed more real than ever, as if the right combination of wishes and alchemy might bring her to life. I wondered again if there was a real woman who looked just like the ice sculpture.

"Who is she?" I asked Shaw.

Shaw said nothing, even though he glanced distractedly in my direction, as if he'd awoken from a nightmare. His eyes darted around then seemed to fix on something in the distance. A painful look appeared in his bloodshot eyes.

I followed his line of sight to see what had him so transfixed and saw a woman in a heavy hooded cloak watching him sculpt from not far off. A sudden gust of wind blew her hood off, exposing her long wavy hair.

It was her! The very woman Shaw had been carving all these years. She was just as beautiful as her frozen image. I glanced at the ice sculpture, confirming that indeed it was the same woman. When I turned to look at the real woman again, she had vanished.

Shaw's shoulders slumped in disappointment, and he turned back to the sculpture.

"It was her!" I shouted at him, my hands shaking from excitement. I dribbled the hot coffee and scorched the exposed skin between my heavy gloves and my jacket wristbands. I bobbled both bagels onto the snow.

Shaw dismissed me with a shrug and went straight back to his carving.

"Who is that woman?" I demanded, my wrists blistering. "Why aren't you going after her?"

Shaw didn't budge. I couldn't believe that he seemed uninterested in seeking out the real woman who inspired and haunted him.

I set off to find her, thinking I saw her in the distance making her way along the riverfront boulevard. She hurried along the sidewalk that edged the top of the river bluff not noticing the steep drop-off just a few footsteps away and the icy and impassable Mississippi below. Another gust of wind sent her cloak flapping, her hair flying. Before I could catch up to her, she disappeared into a crowd gathered around the dreaded Winter Carnival Vulcans—ordinary businessmen who played costumed villains for the annual event—, their faces smudged with soot. These kings of fire symbolized the coming warmer season. Ultimately, they would defeat winter, symbolized by other carnival royalty—King Boreas and his Royal Court—at the end of the carnival.

The mysterious woman had the regal bearing and classic beauty of royalty, and her cloak was of the style of the long capes worn by the carnival royalty, but her otherworldly appearance, so much like her frozen doppelgänger, made it seem like she was from another realm.

My heart began to slow, and as it did, I realized that my wild chase was ridiculous. I looked around to see if Laux had noticed my bizarre behavior, but he was nowhere nearby.

I had been taken in by Shaw's obsession, as if standing so near to him and watching his masterpiece emerge every year had somehow infected me with the same mania. Or perhaps it was a simple matter of the long, hard work of sculpting and the heated competition that was getting to me. I shook it off. I had my own sculpture to finish and needed every minute I had left to get it done.

I laughed at my foolishness. When I walked back to my ice slab, I passed by Shaw and saw him working at his usual pace. He was so absorbed he didn't see me. But I couldn't help but take one last look in the direction where the scarlet-clad Vulcan Crewe devilishly taunted the spectators around them. The mysterious woman was nowhere to be seen.

* * *

I worked nonstop for the rest of the day and late into the evening. It was the last day of the contest and judging would occur early the next morning. Though I could think of a dozen more meaningful touches to make on my sculpture, I was bone tired and growing colder by the minute. The temperature plunged into the single digits with windchills—from the cutting wind—dipping below zero. Except for Shaw, I was the only other sculptor still working on my entry. It was eerily quiet, except for the quiet chipping of Shaw's tools, as all the other sculptor's power tools were shut off. Though I had some battery-powered lights to help illuminate my work area, Shaw worked under the available street-lights, which made it difficult to do all the fine detailing required at this stage, though that never seemed to be a problem for him.

I yawned and shivered, deciding finally to go rest and warm up in my truck for an hour or two before returning refreshed to make the last few changes to my piece. The rules allowed the sculptors to work right up to the judging hour if someone chose, and typical-ly it was the two of us—Shaw and me—who worked through that last night.

I fell asleep quickly in my truck, exhausted by the long hours of work and the strange escapade with Shaw's model. I set the alarm on my cell phone to awaken me by three in the morning but was startled awake by a loud crash outside. I feared some weak spot in my ice sculpture had given way. I hurriedly rubbed the frost of my truck window and looked out to see what had happened.

There was nothing wrong with my piece. I peered through my frosted window in Shaw's direction, squint-ing to see his sculpture in the dim light of the street-lights. I could see what I thought was his sculpture, but then swore I saw it moving. Without a thought, I opened my door and hurried over.

When I heard his sculpture speak, I stopped in my tracks. An agonizing sound came from the woman's throat, a raw pain thawing to tenderness, like frost-bitten limbs warming to life.

She moved, her glassy gown crackling around her, and in a moment was transformed into the same mysterious woman I had seen earlier that day. Yet she was also the same woman he had been carving, over and over for so many years. They had become one and the same. But had the real woman merged with the statue, or had she emerged newborn from the ice, having come to life under the artist's hands?

I saw something flashing in her hand. It was one of Shaw's chisels. Shaw backed away from her, and in doing so tripped over the shards of ice that he had chipped away while sculpting. He fell to the ground heavily, and she dropped to his side.

I crept closer, hypnotized by the beautiful woman bent over the prone sculptor. I swore I heard her say "Darling" to him. And "my love."

And then, "Be with me forever." Then she held the chisel over his forehead and came down on him hard.

I screamed and she saw me. She dropped the chisel, rose to her feet, and disappeared into the midnight shadows of the winter-stripped trees of Kellogg Park.

Shaw lay dead beneath the wreckage of his sculpture.

* * *

Even though I had immediately called 911 to alert the police and tell them the main suspect had gotten away, I was slapped in handcuffs and hauled off.

They questioned me all day and far into the evening. When I told them about the woman I had seen, how she was an exact twin of the sculptures Shaw had carved every year, they laughed.

I repeated my story, never wavering from it, yet never seeming to convince them of its truth.

There were two detectives interviewing me, and they stepped aside to have a brief conversation. The older guy, a slouchy, stained fellow with thinning hair, sent the younger detective out of the room. When he came back not more than twenty minutes later, he showed his boss a photo he'd apparently printed off the web. The old guy nodded and set the picture on the table in front of me.

"That's her," I said, jabbing my finger at the photo. "Who is she? Why aren't you looking for her?"

It was a high quality, black and white photo, a professional shot. The woman was leaning against a blank wall, her head back, her wavy hair cascading around her shoulders, her adoring eyes on the photographer. I knew in a moment that the photographer must be Shaw. Only a man who had experienced that look in her eyes—the look of complete devotion—would be able to render it in sculpture. She was wearing the simple gown Shaw had expertly captured in ice.

When I asked again for the identity of the woman in the photo, the investigators looked at each other, their expressions suggesting I might be insane. Or the worst liar they'd ever encountered.

"Well?" I spoke. "Tell me who she is."

"It's Henry Shaw's wife," the lead investigator said.

"His wife?"

"You heard that right," he said.

"So have you found her yet?" I asked. "Brought her in for questioning?"

The older guy looked like he was about to laugh.

The younger detective answered. "That's not going to happen."

"And why not?" I demanded.

"She's been dead for twenty years."

* * *

Her framed photo sits on a small table in my room, where the light is best. I can see it from almost every angle of my tiny room—it's the first thing I see when I wake in the morning, the last thing I see before falling asleep at night.

I see her in my dreams.

I've been told it would be better for my sanity if the photo weren't displayed so prominently as if it were a religious icon I worshipped. But the one time it was taken away from me, I fell into a deep depression and was moments from committing suicide when the guards stopped me.

I was convicted of killing Henry Shaw—my fingerprints were on the murder weapon. I had picked it up in those initial moments of confusion when I discovered Shaw dead and saw the icy phantom of his deceased wife slipping away. I had hurried out of my truck so quickly that I neglected to put on my buckskin choppers.

Beyond the evidence of my fingerprints, there were enough character witnesses—including Jess Laux—to convince the jury that I was guilty. Laux's testimony was the most damning. He'd said that I'd sworn to kill Shaw to win the contest. In fact, it was Laux who'd come up with the idea of killing Shaw, not me. But my lawyer would not let me take the stand to rebut Laux or any of the other testimony. And once I'd been convicted, my lawyer said the best we could hope for was for me to be committed to an asylum.

He got his wish.

As the years go by, I understand Shaw better and better. Sometimes I think I have become him. I've often sketched his wife's image from memory, and when I do, I think of Shaw sculpting her in ice from memory. When death released him from his obsession, that same obsession was born anew in me. Its grip has been as tenacious as a never-ending winter.

Late at night, I am often awakened from my sleep by what sounds like the north wind rushing through the drafty asylum corridors. And then I swear I see her floating by in her translucent dress, her face glowing under the safety lights, her wavy tresses stirring lightly as she turns to me.

Escapes

At the last minute, Lydia took off her wedding ring and left it behind. She couldn't bear the thought of people noticing the ring, noticing that a husband wasn't along with her on the trip and asking about him, or not asking and just looking at her with pity or accusations or both.

Of course, she had arrived at the justification for removing her ring much later. The moment she removed the ring her mind had been completely blank, the idea spontaneous.

The taxi had been waiting for her at the curb, and she'd remembered that she had wanted to leave her apartment key with her landlord.

"One moment," she had said to the cabbie as he put her suitcase into the trunk. "I forgot something."

She walked up the steps of her apartment one last time and felt in her pocket for her key. She thought of kissing the key goodbye—a silly gesture, to be sure—and felt self-conscious even though the cabbie wasn't paying the least bit of attention and no one else was around. So, she kissed it, and the moment her lips touched the key, she felt her wedding ring brush against her cheek.

Her husband's prognosis had been terminal from the start, yet he had lingered almost two years after the accident, and during those two years, Lydia had given everything away, sold the house, and rented an apartment near the hospital, furnishing it sparely. She told herself she was in limbo during Terrance's long and slow decline, and this was why she hadn't bothered decorating the place. But after he's died and was buried, she immediately bought herself the open train ticket, planning to depart within the week.

She dropped the key into her landlord's mailbox, and on impulse removed her wedding ring, dropping it in her own mailbox with little thought and no regret. The post office was holding her mail, so the ring would lie entombed until she returned. When that would be, she didn't know.

* * *

Lydia showed her train ticket to the porter, and he led her along the shiny train to a two-level sleeper car. She was heading west out of Chicago two thousand miles west across the northern plains, over the Rockies and on to Seattle where she would transfer onto the Coast Starlight and travel along the West Coast for another thousand miles. Once she arrived in San Diego, she'd make her next arrangements. For the moment, she just wanted to let the miles pile up behind her, the cold hard accumulation of distance.

The porter stored her bulky suitcase and led her to a snug, single cabin on the upper deck. As she arranged her things, she took note of the closed upper berth and the two facing reclining seats below that would be converted later into her bed. She was surprised to see a couple in the roomette across from hers, thinking one of the larger rooms might be more suitable for a couple. The man and woman sipped champagne from plastic glasses.

It was two in the afternoon.

"You should have some of the champagne," the woman said.

"Yes, bring her some champagne," the man said to the cabin attendant.

"Of course," the attendant said.

"Bring a few more for us while you're at it," the man said.

The attendant agreed.

"We got kind of crazy last night," the woman explained to Lydia. "On our trip from New York."

"But don't worry, the champagne had nothing to do with it," the man said, with a low chuckle.

The woman gave her companion a seductive nudge, not the least embarrassed, and lifted her glass to his lips as the cabin attendant returned with several bottles. He opened one for Lydia and poured her a glass.

"Please let me know if you need anything else," the attendant said to Lydia, leaving her an extra bottle and distributing the rest to the couple across from her.

"We're on our honeymoon," the woman said. "I'm Nancy and this is Jerry. Second marriage for both of us. And we both just turned fifty too."

They seemed extra motivated to kick off their second half century with gusto. Lydia wondered what she had gotten herself into. Across from a horny, boozy pair of middle-aged honeymooners with just a slender door and a narrow hallway between them.

"Congratulations to you both," Lydia said, lifting her glass. "I'm Lydia." She hadn't drunk so much as a glass of wine in months. She shuddered at the brisk, sweet stink of it, knowing then she'd down both bottles. She more than deserved it.

"It's good to meet you, Lydia," Nancy said as the train began to pull out of the station, "And now, if you'll excuse us…" she added as Jerry slid their door closed. Lydia caught a glimpse of Nancy giving Jerry a wicked smile as he shut their drapes and heard her giggle when he locked the doors, the confinement of a single bed posing no apparent obstacle for their randy attitude. Thankfully, the noise of the station and the track muffled whatever activities were underway in

Cabin F. She wondered whether that would be the case later in the evening.

The steward came by to take note of Lydia's dinner reservation. She'd considered eating alone in her cabin, but the lusty romping across the hallway put a damper on her appetite. She was surprised to find herself so hungry for company.

* * *

"Chris Lewis," the man across the table from her said, shaking Lydia's hand. He was in his mid-thirties, rugged looking, his hair cropped short. A plain elegant watch with an old-fashioned dial adorned his wrist, and his ring finger was bare, though she knew this meant nothing for a man these days. For all she knew, his companion had decided not to join him for dinner. The train was midway across Wisconsin and newly planted farm fields blurred corduroy lines in soft green outside the windows.

She hid her left hand, then remembered the ring wasn't there and placed her hand on the table, relaxing her fingers casually on the linen. It was silly to even think in those terms—she was a recent widow—but she wondered if he noticed the gray hair beginning to shoot through her blond. She hadn't even thought of coloring it yet. Now she regretted not doing it.

"Where are you headed?" he asked.

"Wherever the train takes me, for now," she said, feeling the buzz of fresh alcohol in her system, courtesy of a glass of pre-dinner Merlot. She'd also partaken of the wine- and cheese-tasting with the other first-class passengers in the lounge car, though she didn't join in the conversation but sat with an unread paperback as a prop. Her husband, Terrance, had been the engaging extrovert, energized by extracting minutiae out of everyone, fascinated by even the most mundane nuggets passed along by strangers. Lydia remembered a long conversation he'd had with a mortician at a Chicago restaurant. Terrance chattered with him about embalming as if it had been a lifelong interest of his. They parted practically friends. Terrance was a convenience for an introvert like Lydia. She'd never have an awkward social moment; she'd simply never had to say a word. But now Terrance wasn't there to smoothly handle all the social interactions. She reminded herself that was one reason she was taking the train trip.

So, she'd spent the afternoon getting her bearings, which involved drinking quite a bit more alcohol than she realized. Now that she was ready to chat, she wasn't sure what she wanted to say.

"A free spirit," Chris said. "Cheers," he offered, holding his own glass up. "That's what I love about traveling by train. All the possibilities. I mean, here we are, a cross-section of humanity in this transitional phase of travel, brought together by the coincidence of the dinner hour."

"Transitional," Lydia said. "That perfectly describes where I'm at."

Their conversation was temporarily interrupted as the waiter stopped by to take their orders. Lydia was ravenous, but she wanted to be expansive. She hoped dinner wouldn't arrive too soon.

"Oh?" he said, "What sort of transition?" He smiled.

"I'm between phases in life," Lydia said, not wanting to mention specifics about her husband's death but wanting to keep the man's attention. He looked mildly interested but seemed just as interested in the country landscape out the window, now tinted golden by the angled early-evening light of late spring. He also occasionally glanced in the direction of the line of coach passengers waiting for open tables. Their table had two empty seats—a luxury Lydia was sure.

"There you are," Chris said when a woman his age and a young girl turned up. "I wondered if you were going to join us after all." He introduced his daughter and wife to Lydia, and they slid in, the woman on Lydia's side and the girl next to her father.

"Lydia says she's between phases in life," Chris pointed out.

"Must be nice," Chris's wife said, a little more dismissively than Lydia liked. She noticed the woman glancing at her bare finger and Lydia wondered whether she could see the telltale ridges of skin around her absent ring. She probably thought Lydia was a divorcee on the prowl.

"My husband died a few weeks ago," Lydia said. She regretted saying it the moment it came out of her mouth. The couple immediately expressed their sympathy and Lydia bowed her head, saying a gracious thank you even though she didn't want any more sympathy. That was another reason for taking the trip. She was sick of everyone's sympathy; she'd had more than her share for two years and given her role in the end of his life, she knew she didn't deserve it anyway.

Thankfully, the rest of the dinner didn't require her to speak, as the couple's daughter monopolized their attention. Her first dinner choice was sold out and she pouted through the inferior option.

Lydia left the dining car defeated and spent the rest of the night in her cabin. She was thankful that the stops were brief as passengers departed and arrived, and soon enough it was dark. The one layover around ten in the Twin Cities arrived as many in the sleeper cars were settling in for the night. They set off again, and she tried hard not to think about which squeaks and moans were coming from her neighbors across the aisle or the train itself. She left her window curtains open and focused her attention on the endless lullaby of stars above the northern prairies of western Minnesota and eastern North Dakota.

* * *

Lydia took lunch the next day in her cabin but decided she must try the dining car experience that evening if only to get away from the honeymooners who had slept late into the afternoon, mercifully, but were now rousing themselves.

"Nancy's upset with me," Jerry admitted to her when Nancy went to have a shower and Lydia had stepped into the hallway to tidy up her cabin before heading out to dinner. "Lover's quarrel, I guess," he said.

"We both swore we'd do things different from our first marriages. I don't know, it's been a week, and she already seems tired of me."

Lydia listened patiently without comment as Jerry told her they'd met commuting by train to jobs in Manhattan. One thing had led to another, and two divorces later, they were married to each other.

"You ever been married?" Jerry asked.

Lydia hesitated, then said, "Once."

"Decided once was enough?" Jerry asked, looking exasperated.

"Um," Lydia shrugged, visualizing Terrance laid out in his coffin. She had no idea what his thoughts might have been on her marrying again. Then she wondered why she was even seeking his permission. They'd never talked of such things, as she recalled, though they were romantic lovers once, of course, and they must have talked about who was strong enough to survive the death of the other, the way all lovers do. Had they decided on Lydia? That she was stronger?

Had Terrance given her his blessings to marry again if she were the first to go? She couldn't remember.

She concluded, "I supposed you could say that," noticing Jerry's look of concern. "I'm sure the two of you will work it out," she said, with nothing to go on but their apparent unquenchable lust for each other. She excused herself to go to the dining car just as Nancy returned looking refreshed and smiling.

* * *

Lydia was seated in the dining car with a pair of sisters, both divorcees, who told her that they'd had a cocktail or two (or perhaps three) in their spacious double cabin a few cars beyond the one Lydia was in.

"Isn't this grand," the older of the pair said, raising a toast as the train went over the continental divide near Glacier National Park. Lydia had trotted out the line about being in transition and onto the next phase, then left it at that.

"Here's to Lydia," Sharon said, "on her way to the next phase of her life." The younger sister, a buxom woman just like her sister, tressed in the same cascading waves of black hair, pointed to Lydia's ring finger.

"Looks like your shackles are only recently removed," Gabi said. "A long sentence?"

Sharon shushed her sister. "Don't mind her," she said. "Her husband was way worse than mine. Let's say she has an axe or two to grind."

"Or three! Ha! I'm surprised I didn't kill Bobby," Gabi said. "Even Sharon has said that no court in the world would convict me, the guy was such a jerk."

"Now, now, sis," Sharon said. "Remember? We're on this trip to put that behind us. Her divorce was final just last month. I've been single for years, and even so, I tell Sharon that not everyone is like Bobby. Not everyone is like Rich. Who was, incidentally, *not* rich, if you get my meaning."

Gabi laughed. "That always gets me."

Their dinner orders taken, the women relaxed with a second glass of wine. Sharon glanced at the waiting coach passengers. "Wouldn't it be nice to have a man seated with us?"

"It doesn't look like we have any good candidates," Sharon said. "Plus we're kind of imposing, you know? Three single women on the prowl—right, Lydia?"

"Right," Lydia said, joining in, not knowing what she'd do if someone got seated next to them.

The train made another western Montana stop, and the women watched as a trio of ragged backpackers walked by outside on their way to a coach car. They looked like they'd spent weeks in the backwoods.

"I'm sure they smell like animals," Gabi said, almost hungrily. One of them glanced at the dining car and caught Lydia's eye. She saw him lick his lips, and she turned away, but not before both sisters noticed.

"Looks like Lydia already snagged a boyfriend," Sharon snorted.

"Don't worry," Gabi said, "he's obviously not good enough for you."

"I'll take him on," Sharon said.

"You will not," Gabi said. "Don't be ridiculous."

"Just joking," Sharon said as she watched the men until they were out of sight.

As the train lurched forward, Sharon shook her empty glass at the waiter, and he quickly refilled it.

"So, what's your ideal man?" Sharon said, "if you don't mind my asking."

Lydia thought of Terrance, and what came to mind first was his comatose face, the months and months of sitting next to him in the hospital. He'd been her ideal man, no question—before the accident, of course. Social, dependable, suddenly inappropriately funny with his *sotto voce* comments about strangers. He would have come up with a zinger about these two ladies.

"Someone with a good sense of humor," Lydia said, her voice unexpectedly breaking.

Sharon noticed the start of tears. "Lydia, are we upsetting you or something? My sister can be pretty rude," she said.

"Me?" Gabi said. "You're the one who can't keep a thing to yourself."

Crap, Lydia thought. She'd not wanted this at all. "It's nothing, really," she said, clearing her throat and taking a deep breath. "You know, there are good men out there, Gabi. Though at the moment I want nothing to do with any of them. I just got out of a long-term relationship myself." Specifically, she did not mention her husband's death. "Taking a break from men now." She left it at that.

The two seemed subdued by her remark, but then Sharon piped up. "That's what we're doing too, right Gabi? That's what our trip is all about. Taking a break from men."

The rest of dinner the sisters cackled nonstop with each other, oohing and aahing at the grandeur of the mountains out the window and asking Lydia to keep watch for handsome cowboys. The sisters had quickly forgotten their vow and even caught Lydia up in their discussion, which bordered on bickering in its high-spirited moments.

Lydia had sensations of floating, at times observing herself from that safe distance of a window as if she too had become part of the unfamiliar, gorgeous early evening scenery flashing by. Outside of the person she knew, she looked down at the odd trio, saw herself laughing and joining in. She'd often wondered what Terrance experienced in his comatose state, whether there was some consciousness observing and archly commenting about the predicament the two of them were in.

"Why don't you stop back at our place?" Sharon asked. "The bar's open."

"Been open all day, matter of fact," Gabi said.

"I'd be delighted," Lydia said, swept away by the brassy camaraderie of women she wouldn't ordinarily befriend.

The three women made their unsteady way along the narrow corridors, jostled as the train hit rough tracks. "Ride 'em, cowgirls," Sharon shouted from the lead.

"Woo-hoo!" Gabi said from the rear.

They walked through Lydia's sleeper car, and Lydia nudged both as they walked by Jerry and Sharon's cabin. The shades were open, and the newlyweds leaned into each other, their arms intertwined, watching the sunset drape the rugged scenery with showy glitter.

"Seems they kissed and made up," Lydia said.

"Let's place bets on when they'll have their next tiff," Sharon said after they'd settled into their first drinks in the sisters' cabin.

"Love never lasts," Gabi said. "Right, Lydia?"

"Lydia never said much about her marriage, Gabi," Sharon said.

"That's right," Gabi said. "How'd you put it back there? You're in transition? So, what's your story?"

"Gabi, really."

Lydia felt the buzz of the alcohol—the glasses of wine with dinner, the bottles of champagne beforehand, the dizzying stir inside, the train in constant motion against the magnificent, untouchable backdrop of the mountains.

"I killed him," she said with a hiccup she hoped sounded like a laugh.

The sisters chuckled. "Yeah, right," Gabi bellowed. "That's what my ex used to say," But then she went silent as Lydia refilled her glass.

Lydia knew her face had gone serious, her true character unmasked. "Two years ago," she said, "around this time of year, nice early June night like this one, clear sky, just like now…" She paused, glancing out the window to the darkening vastness of the landscape, the distant snow-covered peaks. "We were on our way home from a night out. He'd had way more to drink, so I said I'd drive." She took another sip. "He told me it wasn't necessary. The guy was a great driver, even with a few in him, but I thought it was best not to take a chance.

"We were on a road we drove every day. I could practically drive it with my eyes closed. Did I mention I hadn't had a thing to drink? I was on a diet, though he was the one who really needed to lose weight. Anyway, that night I'd been determined to stick with it. The diet. Loads of calories in these things," Lydia said, eyeing the plastic cup in her hand. "But of course we're on vacation, so who really cares now."

The train's warning horns sounded as they approached an intersection, and when they passed through, the flashing lights flickered through Gabi and Sharon's room.

"The road narrowed," Lydia continued. "Some road construction had just started up. And another car was merging. I sped up to pass, but the other car sped up too. I don't remember what happened after that. I survived without a scratch. He wound up in a coma and never came out of it."

Lydia finished off her drink, then set her glass down and rubbed her eyes. The dizziness wouldn't go away.

"Hon, it was an accident," Sharon said quickly, her hand on Lydia's arm. "You can't blame yourself for that. It sounds like it was the other person's fault anyway. Didn't you say they were merging? You had the right of way."

Lydia knew there was more to tell—what happened after the accident, the coma that went on and on. She blinked, saw her husband's motionless face, blinked again, and saw the two sisters quietly watching her. They trusted her now. They were sympathetic. She felt the closeness of companionship she had missed. What would happen if she went on with her story? If they heard the whole thing until the end? If she admitted that she hadn't even cried at his funeral. That she grew to hate him.

"Well, that killed the mood," she said lightly, laughing a little.

"Don't you worry about it, Hon," Sharon said. "We're all friends here, right sis?"

"That's right."

Lydia smiled, hoping they found in her face sincere agreement, though she knew she could never be friends with these women, never speak to them again. She'd hoped she could escape the sad fact of what she'd done by taking a trip, getting away with no plans to return. But the miles piling up behind her hadn't changed a thing.

"See you in the morning?" Gabi said as Lydia mentioned it was late, and she'd had a long day. "Well, not too early," Gabi said, laughing. "Let's get lunch together in Seattle."

Lydia didn't mention she'd be changing trains in Seattle.

"Sure," Lydia said. "Sounds great."

* * *

Back in her roomette, the rest of the story replayed itself in Lydia's mind with nothing to interrupt it, nothing to escape from it. The judgmental stars flickered in the night sky. Long after the doctors had said there was no hope, Lydia went on playing the good wife, visiting him almost every day, reading him letters people sent, then rereading the very same letters when fresh correspondence was dropped off. Lydia blamed no one for that. What do you say to a man in an irreversible coma? What do you say to his wife? She just reread everything. He wouldn't have known.

She read his favorite books to him, even though she very often nodded off, then had to reread a few pages to be sure she didn't miss anything, even though she found the books distasteful. He was a fan of true crime, especially those peopled with cruel wives, jealous lovers and murders planned to look like accidents. She had asked him once why he found reading about lowlifes and tramps so appealing. Because, he said kissing her on the forehead, I want to see how the other half lives.

Lydia felt guilty whenever she didn't visit him even though she could accept the fact that he wouldn't have known she had missed a day here or there. At the end of the first year, though she tried hard to ignore it, the resentment began to build for his lingering. For his staying alive. He had never said an unkind thing to her, but his cruel going on tortured her and fed her guilt. Eventually, she accepted that she would have to kill him to be able to go on herself. One of his true crime books offered a method and pointed out the errors made by the killer and techniques for covering up her tracks. No one ever knew.

"You loved him, didn't you?" she would ask herself. "That made it an act of mercy." Surely, even he would understand, being a fan of true crime and believer in the true love in his wife.

She remembered standing at his grave at the end of the services. Everyone was telling her how sorry they were, how tough it must have been for those two years. She couldn't admit to anyone that she wasn't sad he had died. She wasn't. Then it struck her that maybe her lack of grief meant she'd never loved him. And maybe that was why she wasn't sad, wasn't crying. She knew they were saying to each other—but not to her—that it was a blessing he'd finally died. She would have thought the same thing had anyone else suffered her fate. Euthanasia was perfectly legal in some places. Still, shouldn't morality have dictated she wait for nature to take its course no matter how long?

The train pulled up to Spokane at three in the morning, and she was still awake, still wondering again why she'd managed to hate him so much simply because he would not die.

She watched out her window as people boarded the train. In the dead of night, there were no joyous homecomings or happy farewells. Everyone sleepwalked, dragging bulky suitcases. Babies slumped comatose over shoulders, little ones were led along wild-eyed as if in a nightmare. Why hadn't she cried? she kept asking herself. Why had it been so difficult to shed a tear at his funeral?

And why was it so hard to stop now, almost two thousand miles away from where he lay buried?

* * *

The train was making its way into Seattle when Lydia woke from a few hours of troubled sleep. She was so spent from grief that all she could do was stare out the window with stinging eyes as the train performed its autopsy on the great city's industrial innards.

The track cut through an area of reeking refineries and stinking sewage treatment plants surrounded by putrid fields of watery filth, a city digesting and processing its wastes. Next, factories and warehouses came into view, interspersed with aging apartment buildings. The scalpel of the train sliced through the lives of people who could not afford a more distant location from the city's noisy bowels. The streets were stripped bare of niceties like shady boulevard trees, arty bus stops, sidewalk cafes and pretty boutiques. Instead, squatters inhabited junked carcasses of autos no longer mobile, redefining curb appeal as a permanent parking spot in front of a coin-operated laundromat. Rubbish extruded indelicately from the backsides of buildings, hidden from view so that the authorities wouldn't notice but in plain sight of train passengers whose notice didn't matter. Here, life fed on decay, its insatiable appetite consuming every oily morsel.

Lydia debarked the train as quickly as she could at the Seattle station, hoping that the sisters would not see her scurrying away. She hurried to the platform where her connecting train was already boarding, impatiently holding up her ticket to the porter. Within moments, she was aboard her next train, locking the roomette door behind her and closing the hallway window curtains.

Her west-facing room would give her a good, long look at the Pacific. She wondered whether she would be able to distinguish the vanishing point of horizon that divided the pale blue ocean from the pale blue sky.

Perpetua

The deafening rumble of the Harley disturbed the quiet contemplation of the nuns in the Benedictine convent house. Sister Perpetua alone embraced the hog. She knew it seemed wrong to ignore part of her monastic vocation—to revere silence. Instead, she cherished the motorbike's chanting cadence, the thrill that burned through her body. To Perpetua, the Harley's voice came from God. What else could explain her burning desire to seek it out, feel the wave of mercy it bestowed. She felt blessed by the Savior, so she never confessed her peculiar interpretation of God's transcendent calling.

When the summer heat shimmered, she boldly took another risk. Alone in her room, she removed the oppressive nun's habit and waited quietly by her window—chastely clad in demure, virginal underclothes and alert to every sound in the neighborhood that surrounded the convent.

Late one night, she fell asleep in her chair until the distant sound of the Harley woke her. She strained to see through the darkness, hear its approach. That night, the hog throbbed softly, and as it neared the convent, it began to slow, coming to a stop not far from her window.

She could see the helmeted rider who was looking directly at her. She silently left her room, glided out the front door, and slipped across the front lawn, ready to be embraced by the Savior. In the dim streetlight, she saw her face reflected in the rider's black visor.

Perpetua ached to see the rider's face but knew she couldn't ask. Would God answer her prayers? When the rider's face was revealed at last, Perpetua shivered in ecstasy. The rider handed her the helmet and motioned for her to take a seat.

* * *

Sister Perpetua held the helmet for a long time, her hands shaking slightly. When she handed it back to the rider, she whispered, "Who are you?"

Standing before her was a woman—not that the Lord can't be a woman, Perpetua knew. But why did her face look so familiar?

The rider got off her machine, took Perpetua's hand and led her to the nearest streetlight. She situated them so their faces were brightly lit, then positioned the helmet's visor to act as a mirror. Perpetua glanced at the rider who was gazing at the mirror.

The woman appeared to be close to Perpetua's present age of thirty-three.

"Behold," the rider inaudibly conveyed through a series of pleasurable waves sent ripping through Perpetua.

The nun looked in the mirror and saw a single face—her own—until the rider made a slight adjustment to the angle of the visor. Then two identical faces came into view, and Perpetua wondered at the optical illusion, like the kind created in a carnival's hall of mirrors.

Unlike the other nuns, Perpetua loved the crowds, dust, and noise of the county fair. She quickly slipped away from the fair's multi-denominational chapel to head to the funhouse. The perpetuating visions were sinfully intoxicating, even though they were sometimes grotesque. The carneys let her stay as long as she liked. Her habitual appearance became part of the attraction they luridly pitched, drawing in customers who crept by Perpetua with shrieks and giggles.

Was her experience of the Savior nothing more than a funhouse maze of mirrors? What was the Messiah trying to tell her with this curious vision?

Just then one face in the mirror turned to the side, while the other looked straight ahead. Perpetua gasped.

The Lord and Savior Jesus Christ was her twin.

* * *

But not a twin. For there was one difference between her and the Biker—an irreverence for silence. The Biker tossed her helmet aside, mounted her Harley, and gunned the engine. An apocalyptic din reverberated through the neighborhood, broadcasting lusty echoes off the nearby cathedral.

The Biker glanced at her discarded helmet and then eyed Perpetua with a challenging look. The Rider announced her imminent departure with another loud howl from her machine.

Lights flickered on inside the convent house and began to throw damning omens onto the lawn. Shadowy figures gathered behind the windows.

The convent door creaked open.

The Biker pulled her machine away from the curb. A moment later, Perpetua snatched the helmet and leaped onto the Harley, clinging tightly to her Savior. They fled into the darkness, the bike accelerating when they left the town.

They sped across the roller-coaster countryside, thrilling nausea accenting every transition from descent to ascent. They entered a narrow, twisted river valley as dawn curved through the coulees and lit the river bluffs and the towns. The bike swiftly stitched the winding seam of land and shimmering river.

At last, the Harley slowed and came to a stop along the main street of a tiny riverside village.

"Come, Sister," the Biker said, taking Perpetua's hand and leading her inside a cottage. Stilts held the back half of the house above a steep embankment. Just below the house, railroad tracks edged the riverbank and a wide expanse of water mirrored the empty blue sky.

"Put these on," the Biker commanded, handing Perpetua duplicate sets of the clothing she wore. Perpetua shed her chaste lingerie and clad herself in biker gear. "Now go," the Biker said, pushing her out the door and handing her the keys to the place.

* * *

On the horizon every sister from the convent stood armed to the teeth. In their alabaster hands they brandished clubs, bicycle chains, and crucifixes ripped from the walls and sharpened on all points.

The vestal virgin apocalypse—their smothering cloaks flying and menacing weapons raised high—closed in around Perpetua. Mother Superior shot through their ranks, her black habit spreading behind her like expended rocket fuel from a missile.

Perpetua's head dropped in customary obeisance until the animal smell of the black leather snapped her to. Her Savior stepped out clad in Perpetua's demure former self as the nuns tightened their ranks. Suffocating darkness and stern faces blocked any escape.

The Rider clutched Perpetua's arm and transferred the Savior's supernatural power through Perpetua, shocking her heart and soul. Perpetua staggered back—the earth threatening to swallow her—as the mystical current hotly purified her being.

Dazzling light radiated through her every pore. She sheltered her twin and withdrew a slender silver dagger from her boot, holding it high in the light emanating from her. Its brilliant reflection sliced first across Mother Superior's throat and then spread its threat across the throats of the rest of the nuns.

"Back you sinners!" Perpetua roared at the nuns.

The squadron of holy women fell back at the sight of the armed, vengeful woman with the otherworldly voice. All knew of the long line at daily confession. Even Mother Superior was impure. Her online gambling had nearly bankrupted the convent house, her cover-up had almost cost her high position, but her appetite for dominance knew no bounds. She used her knowledge of the high cardinal's undisclosed sex crimes to keep her power.

"The heretic must die!" Mother Superior cried, spinning her weaponized rosary to signal the charge.

* * *

And die she did, but with each death a resurrection followed until the angels rolled the moon in front of the sun. The woman in white dropped to her martyred twin's side, pressed her lips against her sister's bloodied mouth and inhaled her last breath. She wailed, her sorrow multiplying and transecting the wide river valley.

The warrior nuns—struck dumb by an eerie midday night and the resounding grief—littered the street with their dropped weapons. They collapsed like disgraced telescopes with shoddy lenses. They shoved and pushed and fought with each other to climb aboard a fleet of awaiting school buses. Once inside, they clutched rosary beads and mumbled Marian prayers to justify what they'd just done. The chorus lapsed into another recitation of holy excuses, their ugly victory yielding another vulgarity to deny.

Vengeful spirits flew in on the wings of innumerable birds of prey. Claws and beaks lifted the crimson-stained weapons and released them to bomb the departing vehicles. Even when the buses were well out of town, the punishing din of metal and stone hitting the buses, the war cries of the birds, and the beseeching screams of the nuns could be heard. At last, the birds returned, circling the moon until it released the sun.

Inside the cottage, the twin removed Perpetua's bloodied clothing, washed her body gently, and wrapped her with a pair of gossamer curtain sheers. After pulling her sister's torn riding gear on, the Rider fastened an ironing board to the back of the Harley and secured the lifeless Perpetua to it by wrapping several more translucent curtains around her and the ironing board until only Perpetua's blood-drained face could be seen.

And then there was nothing left to do but douse the inside of the cottage with lighter fluid, toss in a match, and drive off as it exploded in flames.

* * *

But the story of Perpetua spread from convent to convent. One-by-one, nuns began to lose their composure, began straining to hear a single Harley prowling the neighborhood late at night. Their desires were answered by sleepless nights of seemingly eternal silence.

A search for the Rider commenced. Wanted posters bearing the photo of Perpetua's face—the Rider's twin—were tacked to church bulletin boards, printed in Sunday circulars. Every sermon ended with an order to parishioners to hunt her down. Church authorities claimed they wanted the anti-Christ brought to justice. Schools of study began to form under the auspices of the bishops and cardinals, and new chapters were added to the holy books.

While the debates flared, the nuns remained uninvolved. Should there be a following, they wondered? With no sign of the Rider, no one could answer the question. Who exactly was Perpetua? Had she been the chosen one at the time of her death, the Rider's supernatural powers having transformed her? If that were so, perhaps Perpetua lived on in the form of the Rider.

Throaty thrumming—a cadence of basal moans—emerged from the convent rooms. This singing chorused first into a hymn of loss: the suppressed promise of unwitnessed women. Gradually it built, spilled into the hallways, out of the windows. Passers-by stood bewitched by the eerie music. The raw song swelled, echoed against the churches and cathe-drals, disrupted services. Its persistent Harley heartbeat overpowered the sound of church bells, resounding through towns, frightening some, enraging others, but empowering many to join the call.

Nuns began to leave convents, suit themselves in leather and drive Harleys.

It was the only way to understand Perpetua. Their one real chance to be embraced by the grace of the Savior meant being witnessed, witnessing. Salvation was in that empowering roar you owned atop a Harley.

Everlasting Light

Edwina lay in her coffin and considered everlasting light. Given that she now had an eternity to think on such things, she took her time. Decades passed by in no blink of her eye—she could no longer blink—as she lay silently contemplating eternity.

Her subject matter was close at hand, inescapable, all that light glazing her in a patina of blessed permanence.

She did not want to cloud her thoughts by asking for her husband's opinion, which would have been simple to do because he lay in the coffin right next to hers. What anniversary was it? Their hundredth? Or did the clock stop when he'd died sometime after their fifty-sixth anniversary? When she died a few months after what would have been their seventy-fifth?

She tried hard to remember—to count the moments, the birthdays, the silver and golden anniversaries. But it was getting harder and harder to bring it all back. She had memorized poems as a child, reciting them perfectly well into her nineties, but now she could only recall scattered fragments. She began to think of Emily Dickenson's "There's a certain Slant of light, Winter Afternoons that oppressed ..." then lost the rest. What had that light oppressed? Then it came to her "...Heavenly Hurt," and she realized then what it was about the heavenly light of the hereafter that bothered her so much.

She recalled a trip she and her husband, then newlyweds, had taken to witness a solar eclipse. They'd travelled several hundred miles to watch the moon occult the sun and observe a few moments of nether-worldly darkening.

She wanted to ask her husband what he remembered from that trip, perhaps now a century ago, or possibly a millennium? She didn't know exactly when it had been. Eternity expanded around her with no past and no future, unfolding in continuity, not keeping time by a calendar or a clock.

She decided not to ask him. She couldn't count on him to reconstruct *her* memories, anyway. He had his own to keep track of. It was up to her to remember, to dig under the layers of infinity gradually forgetting her entire life.

She remembered they had driven all day and most of a night and slept on the hard floor of the van at a rest stop, making love inside the van even though she was both unnerved and thrilled by the flashes of light from passing cars. She was afraid they might be seen, yet delighted by the thrill of having her passion witnessed. The next day, the escapade made her bold enough, to initiate sex in broad daylight when they had parked in the river town where they planned to watch the eclipse.

He made her stop. She remembered him glancing out the window, a look of embarrassment reddening his face.

"No one cares," she'd said, hoping to change his mind. "No one will even notice," she added, though it was the thought of someone possibly noticing that made the idea so enticing.

"We don't want to miss the eclipse," he had said, kissing her on the forehead and hurrying out. She bit her lip hard, tasted the metal in her blood.

The light had already begun to dim, tinting the landscape in honey.

They stood on the riverbank, holding homemade contraptions over their eyes to shield them and allow them to see the moon as it swallowed the sun, the lunar mouth opening wide to taste a blood orange. The light thickened, went tawny then ochre, and even the birds went silent thinking that evening had arrived.

When the moon fully covered the blood-red sun, an orgasmic corona throbbed around them.

Minutes later the moon began to spit out the blood orange as if it had been too bitter, or too tangy, for its blander taste. Soon after, the sky brightened and the birds chirped again as if nothing more than another morning had arrived.

They returned to the van, and Edwina remembered thinking she might try again. Had she? She couldn't remember. In the steady light of infinity, she could no longer remember the fleeting moments of her life—the sharp taste of a blood orange, the wet exploration of a first kiss, and even the momentary disappointments of love. All the transitory moments she knew as her life on Earth was fading.

And that was exactly what she missed, those brief pleasures and painful disappointments that made you who you were, that told you who you loved.

She thought of asking her husband whether he still loved her. Did she still love him? They had promised to love each other for eternity, but eternity had not agreed to a bargain they had made on Earth. She lay, bathed forever in light, longing for love.

Tonic

Clem woke to a milky blaze, certain it came from one of the floodlights of their apartment building parking lot in Houston. She sat up in the back seat—an acidic hum drilling her REM-interrupted brain—and when she saw thick clusters of stars lighting up a country sky, she knew she was mistaken. It was the middle of the night, and they were in the middle of nowhere, far from Houston. But where?

It had been Jace's idea to drive to Mexico and back in one day, and he had it in his head to hit all the border towns while they were living in Houston waiting for his parole to end.

One border town a week would be a hoot, he'd said. Help them to pass the time. Piedras Negras—only a four-hour drive along Highway 10—was the obvious first choice. Jace liked the sound of it so much he celebrated by downing a six-pack of Negro Modelo that he'd purchased instead of the soda he'd said he had bought for their trip.

Clem had pointed out that drinking beer was a parole violation.

It wasn't American beer, Jace had said. It didn't count.

Would crossing the border be a parole violation, she worried?

Jace said they'd keep a low profile, laughable given his 250-pound, six-foot-five physique, which he crowned with a several-sizes-too-small porkpie hat. She was a foot and a half shorter, 150 pounds lighter, and growing thinner by the day, given everything Jace had put her through.

"You doubt my ability to slip unnoticed into Mexico, darlin?" he had said sucking down the last of the six-pack. He gave her a beery hug. "Come on, we need a madcap adventure. I'm going nuts sitting around all day long."

He had told her that parole made it impossible for him to find work, but it gave him plenty of time to strum his twelve-string, and he promised Clem he'd write songs that would make him a star, songs just like the one he played the night he'd met her. His baritone voice was doped up with dulcet tones of hope, and she instantly fell for that tonic sound, planting faith despite all evidence to the contrary. His optimism always led to dead ends, but that never bothered him. Why should it bother her?

* * *

"I think I made a wrong turn," Jace said, flicking the ash from his cigarette out the window.

"We're lost?" she asked.

Jace shrugged and gave her an apologetic smile.

"Great," Clem said. "How long have we been here?"

"A half hour," Jace said. "Maybe. I thought I'd better let you sleep if you needed to." He held the cigarette out to her. She shook her head.

She continued glancing between the dash clock and the night sky to sort out the situation. They'd made it to the Mexican border in the middle of the afternoon when a triad of emotions—disappointment, irritation, relief—first hit that day. That trio had long juiced their relationship, a song Clem thought of as her love for Jace. Lately, she'd gotten stuck in disappointment and irritation. A chord without a high note was no tonic.

"We got here," Jace said, when they learned that passports would be required to cross the border, passports they did not possess. "That was the goal!" he said, using one of her words—goal—not his. When that didn't work he tried another note. "Let's celebrate!" Clem knew they were going to celebrate whether she wanted to or not.

Jace's idea of a celebration was a leisurely dinner and drinks at the nearest dive, and that meant they headed back to Houston far later than Clem thought they should. Now they were lost, and who knew whether they would get back at all.

Jace got out of the car and Clem climbed into the front seat looking for the carefully arranged maps she'd left on the passenger side. "I'll map with my phone," he'd said, patting the chest pocket of his t-shirt.

"Works fine until you run out of signal," Clem had said, tiling three maps across the passenger seat.

"Don't worry about it," Jace had told her. "It's a straight shot with one easy turn."

Only Jace could miss the one easy turn. Only Jace could convince her to drive halfway across Texas and back in one day and take the wheel with the heavy smell of booze on his breath when Clem started to fall asleep at the wheel. Only Jace could give her a wink and a quick hug, ladle on his easy Oklahoma charm, and juice her out of the toxic triad into a plateau of hopefulness.

The array of maps was gone, replaced by a pile of empty cellophane wrappers for little chocolate donuts, Jace's favorite junk food treat. Clem didn't remember bringing any junk food from Houston. A glob of maps wedged open the glove compartment, likely jammed in there the moment she nodded off in the back seat.

A thunder crack lifted Clem off the car seat. Moments later, Jace stood next to the open car window with a gun in his hand and an even goofier grin on his face.

"Sum bitch. Helluva kick, Clemmy. Wanna try?"

"Where did you get that?"

"Found it by the side of the road here," he said, kicking the gravel to emphasize the veracity of his claim.

"No, I don't want to try. Put that thing back where you found it and get in the car." Clem studied the maps for only a moment longer until she saw oncoming flashing lights in the rearview mirror.

Jace dropped the gun to his feet and nudged it under their car with the side of his foot just as the squad car pulled up behind them. Clem slid over into the driver's seat instinctively.

An officer stepped out of the squad and walked to their car's driver side window. His eyes fixed on Jace's first, then he leaned in, and Clem saw him note the position of the front seat – pushed way back, and her—all five-foot-zero-inches of her—far away from the gas and brake pedals.

"Ma'am, do you mind stepping outside of the car so I can have a word with you and the gentleman over there?"

Clem slid back across the seat and got out of the passenger side door, taking a deep breath of the night air to discern how much alcohol could be smelled on Jace's breath.

"Good evening, officer," Jace said. "What a beautiful night. All those stars sure light the place up. I've been telling Clem here to get out and check it out."

"Where are you folks headed?" he asked.

"We're just passing through on our way home to Houston," Jace said, always faster with a friendly-sounding explanation.

"We got lost," Clem said as brightly as she could. "Pulled over to look at the maps and figure out where we turned wrong." She hoped the cover of darkness hid the telltale heat in her face, but Jace was right. The stars shined on them like nothing she'd ever seen, and now the lights of the squad car were spotlighting them even more. Clem wondered if the gun was visible given all that light, but he couldn't chance looking down to see if that was the case.

"Maybe you can point us in the right direction," Jace said, closer to the officer than Clem thought prudent.

"Can you tell me who was driving?" he asked.

"I was?" Clem spoke, unable to avoid the unsure lift at the end of her statement. She had been driving. Just not right then.

"She definitely has a better sense of direction than I do," Jace said, layering on a plausibility of detail.

The cop gave Jace the once-over and shot another glance through the car window, registering the denial of a front seat pushed back so far that Clem would have had to wear stilts to reach the gas pedal. Clem knew the cop was exaggerating each move, proving to them he knew what was going on, and setting them up for an eventual confession were Clem or Jace to crack.

The sweet smell of Jace's breath hung in the night air. Another DWI would send him back to jail for even longer than his last one.

"A rancher out here said he'd heard a gunshot a short while ago. Do you folks know anything about a gun shot?"

"I thought I smelled cattle," Jace said with a look of wonder. "Maybe there're rustlers around. Giddy up!"

"I was inside, looking at the maps, until you pulled up," Clem said. At least that was true. Clem wondered if she could accept the fact that it would be her fault if Jace got off this time. She didn't want the responsibility of making that decision. But why was it her responsibility at all? She was no judge, no jury.

"Can you point us the way to Houston?"

"You're headed to the border," the cop said after a pause. "Houston's the other way. Just turn around, go back through town, and you'll find the highway entrance right on the other side. Can't miss it."

"Can't miss it unless you're me, right Clem?" he said, punctuating the statement with a whiskey-scented belch.

"Idiot," Clem couldn't help saying.

"Excuse me?" the cop said.

"Oh, I didn't mean you…" Clem said, "…sir."

"The alcohol is pouring off this guy. Were you really behind the wheel?" The cop asked her. "That seat," he said, "is positioned for a guy his size and not yours."

He was making it so easy for her. Like Jace was more his problem than hers, and he'd happily take Jace off her hands. The cop took a step closer to Clem, ignoring Jace as if he were a misbehaving child.

"I just left the scene of a robbery. The thief got away, but no one got a description of the car or the license plate number. The owner had fallen asleep and was clocked on the side of the head right as he woke up. A rancher said he heard a gun go off, a big one, maybe a .357, which matches the description of the gas station owner's stolen gun. Are you sure you haven't heard anything? Seen anyone else passing through?"

"Oh, now that's terrible," Jace said, as if the cop's dearest relative had unexpectedly died. "I do remember hearing a noise but can't be sure. Maybe over there?" he said pointing off into the dark. No one bothered to look where Jace had pointed.

The cop shook his head. "I need your drivers' licenses."

* * *

Clem knew the cop would quickly confirm why Jace's license was suspended. Maybe then he'd insist on a Breathalyzer test that only Clem would pass. Jace's future would be decided for her.

"Darlin'?" Jace quietly said while the cop sat in his car. He tried to strum her past the irritation, past the disappointment. "Help me out here."

"Where did you get that gun?" Clem asked.

"I found it, just like I said. Found it in a gas station restroom. A ways back. Someone stupider than me left it there. I figured, well, maybe someone was going to get hurt if it just sat there."

"How'd you pay for the donuts?" she asked, knowing that she controlled all the money, since Jace couldn't be trusted with a dime.

"I found some money. Left it on the counter. Didn't want to wake the poor guy."

"You *found* some money," she said. "You *found* it?"

"Darlin', it's me. Big dumb old Jace," he said. "I make dumb mistakes, I know. I swear it was all an accident."

The cop walked back to the two of them.

"Your license is suspended," he said to Jace. "I'm sure you both know why. But yours is fine," he said, giving Clem another chance to tell the truth. Another chance to relieve herself of Jace, of that toxic tonic that only he could create.

She said nothing.

"I'm letting both of you go with a warning since I can't cite you for poor seat alignment. Are you," he said looking at Clem, "are you sure you don't know anything about a gun going off around here?"

Clem knew the gun under the car would tell the police everything they needed to know. But she might wind up an accessory if Jace really had been responsible for the robbery. It was past the point where she could point a finger without having it pointed back at her.

"So, Houston is that way?" Clem asked.

"That's all you have left to say?"

"It's what I need to know," she said.

"Yes," he said. "Houston is that way. Please, just get in your car and get going. I don't want to see either of you in this county again."

"Thank you, sir," Jace said, his head hanging down. "Appreciate it."

Jace opened the passenger door and Clem got inside, sliding over into the driver's seat, knowing she had to live with its poor positioning until they were far enough away.

Jace leaned down to get in next, grabbing the gun the moment the cop's back was turned, and stuffing it under the passenger seat.

Clem made a U-turn and drove past the squad car. Jace nodded at the cop as they drove by.

"I'm sorry, darlin'," Jace said once they were far enough away. "I got hungry and stopped at the gas station and used the restroom. Guy was asleep, and honest-to-Pete, all I wanted was some chocolate donuts but didn't have any money because you never let me have any money. The guy left his gun sitting on the counter next to him, and when he started to wake up, I grabbed his gun and hit him with it before he saw me."

"It's my fault you robbed a gas station?"

"I didn't take much," he said. "I didn't hit him that hard."

Clem said nothing.

"I left enough to pay for the donuts," he said.

"As if that makes it all OK," Clem said. "Paying for stolen food with stolen money."

They drove for a while, then came to a small town.

"Is that the place?" Clem asked, seeing a gas station on the edge of town. Several squad cars were out front.

"Looks like it," Jace said, "But I can't be sure. It's awfully dark out here."

"Awfully dark?" Clem said. "Right." Clem pulled into the parking lot and left the motor running. "Get out," she said.

"Now darlin', really?" Jace said.

"I said get out. I meant it."

"I'm sorry," Jace apologized, giving her the biggest smile yet. He retrieved the gun that he had stuffed under the passenger seat, holding it low enough so she could clearly see he was pointing it at her but not revealing his threat to the cops.

"I can't do that," he said. "Just drive out of here as nicely as you please, darlin'."

"Go ahead," she said, turning off the ignition. "Shoot me in the parking lot of the gas station you just robbed, right in front of a half-dozen police officers."

Jace shoved the gun back under the seat, saying "I was just kidding, darlin'." Her eyes locked on his as the sweat began to pour down from under his porkpie hat.

"I'm not," she said. "Either shoot me or get out of the car."

"I'm not leaving," Jace said. "Clem, we gotta get out of here before the cops get suspicious."

Clem saw the terror in Jace's eyes, and the sight of it made her feel calmer than she had in years. She had so many options, so many avenues to be free of him at last. Jace had threatened to kill her, he had been driving drunk, a Breathalyzer would easily prove.

"Clem?" Jace pleaded quietly. "Won't you give me one more chance? Please, darlin'?"

The cop who'd just questioned the two of them pulled into the gas station parking lot.

"Give me the money you stole," she said, grabbing her purse from the back seat. Jace reached behind the seat for the plastic bag where he'd stuffed the cash with the mini donuts. "Put the gun in there, too."

Jace did as he was told.

Clem took the keys out of the ignition and dropped the bag containing the stolen cash, uneaten mini donuts, and the gun into her purse.

She opened the car door. "I'm going in to use the restroom. Stay here."

Ten long minutes later, Clem came back, got into the car, and started it. It wasn't until they were within a half-hour of Houston that Clem next spoke, telling Jace she'd put the gun, the money, and the mini-donuts Jace had taken into the men's restroom trash.

"They have everything back, and since I prepaid for gas that I didn't pump, I've more than covered the donuts you took and paid for with stolen money."

She pulled up to a bus stop just on the outskirts of Houston and left the car running. "You get out here," she said. "Take this," she said, pulling out his emergency whiskey bottle, "and get out of my life." She opened her wallet and handed him a hundred dollars, knowing it wouldn't get him far, especially how he was with money.

"You don't really want this," Jace said, "Darlin'?"

Clem focused her gaze on the haze of city lights—lights that had blotted out the sea of starlight they'd seen in the countryside. "Yes, I do," Clem said, numb with hope.

Jace began to sing softly, his baritone vibrating through her as if she were a tuning fork he was trying to sound. The healing apology of his song worked its way around her and then through her, until she forced herself to leave the car, leaving Jace to the hollow wail of his gorgeous song.

Boys will be Boys

Arvo Thorson sat on his dead mother's chintz armchair one windless July night. For hours, he kept watch out her bedroom window, seeming to take in nothing more than the brooding mirror of Lake Superior.

His handgun rested on his knee.

The house had been his alone since his mother's death the summer before. His father had abandoned the family so long ago that no one bothered looking him up. Arvo himself hung back a year before finally driving north from Minneapolis to Tofte to lay claim to it. He'd stopped in town to pick up a few groceries—white bread, cold cuts, and jerky—when the cashier told him what she'd heard about the place being haunted.

Arvo scoffed.

"She didn't tell you about those kids cutting through her yard?" the clerk asked.

Arvo said no. Kids had been cutting through her yard to get to the narrow, rocky point that arched into the lake. This was nothing new to Arvo—kids growing up in Tofte had always hiked out to the point for late night drinking parties.

"It got really bad last summer. They were throwing rocks at her house, trashing her yard. I told her she should call you. But she would just shrug it off saying, 'Boys will be boys.'"

Last summer. The summer she'd had the coronary, then died.

"Now those kids are going around swearing the place is haunted," the clerk said. "Truth was, *they* were doing all the haunting last year. Probably scared her to death."

Arvo felt the shame rushing to his neck, flooding his face. He was a cop. He'd seen a lot of cruelty and grown plenty cynical. Seeing the same people commit the same crimes again and again. The victims were inconvenient, interchangeable cogs who caused a lot of paperwork. He sometimes forgot to have tissue on hand for their tears. Sometimes he didn't bother following up. Open casework overflowed his inbox and puddled on his office floor. He hid his incompetence with eruptions of arrogance.

But this time it was his mother. His house. She hadn't called. Had she guessed he might blow her off? He would have. They both knew it.

* * *

He drove through his hometown and made it to the little vacant house at the harbor's edge. He saw the battered siding and the empties on the overgrown flower garden his mother had so carefully tended. He closed his car in the garage before letting himself inside to sit in the dark at his mother's bedroom window. His finger toggled his gun's safety on and off.

The lake had grown sharp and stainless when he first heard boys' voices.

Arvo heard a crash—glass breaking. He didn't move. His finger rested on the safety.

He felt another thud against the house. Then laughter. The voices grew distant and still Arvo remained where he was. He'd been on enough stakeouts to know how to wait, how to be silent.

Arvo kept watch as the boys' bonfire shot sparks on the point. Stars flickered and burned acid pinholes across the black gut of sky. At midnight, a sudden wind shattered the vast lake into countless jagged edges.

Arvo sensed his mother's panic. It seeped out of her broken, musty chair and twitched on his skin. Yes, he should have known. Boys will be boys.

Hours later, the bonfire died in the chilling air. Soon after that he heard boys' voices heading his way. He toggled the safety switch once more and stood silhouetted by the moon at the window watching them come ever closer. Soon they were close enough that Arvo could make out their faces in the bright moonlight. He thought he saw one glance in his direction and he froze, the gun in his hand. The boy looked away without noticing the police officer standing in the front of the bedroom window, a gun pointed directly at him.

Boys will be boys.

The boys passed by directly below Arvo, then turned at the corner of the house, and while Arvo could no longer see them, he heard the crunch of the gravel driveway under their feet, their voices echoing off the lake, but growing more distant and muffled as they made their way to the county road.

Another moment for action had come and gone, and Arvo had done nothing. The dead weight of his unused weapon made him grow more ashamed by the moment. He flipped the safety on and locked it away in a cabinet.

When all had at last grown quiet outside, he listened intently to the stillness within the empty house, sensing all the care his mother had put into the place. He could feel her presence in every creak of the floor, sense her tidy hand ordering and organizing everywhere. He flipped through the pages of her daily calendar and examined the neat writing of her daily to-do list, each day's activities noted and checked off in pencil. The very last entry she had made showed two tasks that hadn't been completed. Put the garbage out in the morning, one read. Sort recycling, read the other.

Without another thought, he located empty garbage bags and a heavy pair of work gloves, both neatly stored exactly where they had been kept for decades. He headed outside, where countless glass shards sparkled like treacherous cresting waves in the moonlight.

In the Margins

"She was tiny and thin, with yolk-colored hair and albumen skin," the director had dashed off in the margin. She was the only patient, or more accurately, inmate, admitted to "The Asylum for the Dangerously Insane" on that day.

Today such places are known as state hospitals, a name as sanitizing as a doctor's coat, but back then it was suitably condemned by its original name, apt for a chain-gang of snow-crusted buildings in a pitiful landscape.

She had been sent there after pleading guilty to being a drug-addicted, neglectful, unwed mother and after surrendering me, her infant daughter, to the authorities. She was seemingly absorbed like a vapor into the toxic population of murderers, molesters, and madwomen. I searched for her many years later, and she stubbornly remained an elusive specter. The odd description was the first tangible indication she had been a flesh and blood woman. But why had her appearance caused a singular mention in the margin—a broken egg spilled at the edge of a page? I had to know more.

* * *

The first time I heard her name I was a teenager, and I was told it would be the only time I'd hear it, so I wrote it down in my diary as soon as I could.

I had immediately demanded more details as I knew it would be my one chance. Mother wasn't much for small—or any other—talk.

"I thought you should know her name," she said.

She wouldn't even say the word adopted. She spoke a name and nothing else.

I begged for more.

"You don't want to know more," she said.

I threatened to run away. Mother wasn't ever known to give a direct look. But right then she did, looking me full in the face, her expression hostile. Was she evaluating whether I was ready to hear the truth? Or feeling threatened? Another mother might have grown teary when forced to admit that the child she had raised was another woman's. The longer she looked at me, the angrier she got. Didn't she know what was best for me? Was my questioning an affront to her parental judgment?

It was then I learned about the asylum—that I'd been taken from my birth mother just before she had been committed. Mother and Father received a knock at the door one winter night, and child-abandonment officials handed me to them. Mother and Father were childless and had contacted the county hoping for just such a situation. Papers were drawn up listing them as my parents and a guessed-at birthdate from the summer before.

"You don't need to know more," Mother told me. She didn't know much more herself, she claimed, though I'd heard a few muffled conversations between Mother and Father—about "her." I never learned more, not the age she was when I was born (was she barely more than a teen herself? already middle-aged?) and certainly not what she looked like. I took special notice of women who resembled me, women who were completely unlike the tall, ruddy-complexioned people who raised me. I watched for women with pale yellow hair and skin that sunburned easily. But I never detected any of them taking special notice of me.

During a frenzied moment a year or so later, I tore out a chunk from my diary—some boy had broken my heart and I was determined to erase him, forgetting I'd tucked her name in between pages of teenage drama about my first love. I lost her then and tried hard later to recall her name. Was she named after a flower? Lily? Rose? Was her last name an occupation? Taylor? Wheeler? An unpronounceable town in the old country? Nothing sounded right.

For years, that was all I had, a half-remembered name, fragments of my birth story, stern reminders from Mother that we would never speak of her again. I determined I'd have to go it alone and began to formally search for her when I was living on my own, but I was immediately denied access to my own birth record and any death records at the county courthouse. Without a date, without a birth certificate listing both of our names or any other official record that connected us, I left empty handed. I even combed the census records from the time, but never recognized a name that could have been hers.

Even the asylum wasn't giving up anything else about her. It had long been shuttered, its tragic secrets locked behind a high fence and an electronic security system. I knew there was a cemetery on the grounds, but so many inmates had been buried in unmarked graves that even if I'd been allowed in, I would have learned nothing. I searched through old phone books in the town library where the asylum was located, soon giving up as there were so many names, and so many years had come and gone.

* * *

I found the adoption papers when I was boxing up Mother and Father's things after Mother died at eighty, ten years after Father had passed. My hands shook as I read and reread my birth mother's name, the date she formally gave me up, and my birth name. Finally, I could narrow down my search, so I started over, searching the census records and phone books once again, but still not finding her. Had she never left the asylum? Never gone on with her life somewhere else?

I learned that with special clearance I could look at the asylum director's journals, which were kept in a secure library at the county courthouse. The adoption papers were enough to grant me the clearance I needed. I paused then. For a year, then another, driving passed the sturdy brick courthouse building more than once, stopping out front, and panicking at the thought of climbing the solid concrete stairs and going inside. Maybe Mother had been right, as stern as her judgment sounded so many years before.

"You don't want to know more."

I was afraid of learning too much, too little, or nothing at all. Each option seemed equally damning. I had stopped short of many other important decisions in my life. Men came and went. The chance to marry and raise my own family passed me by. I told myself that it was because I didn't know that I could not take any risks. Because maybe I was too much like my birth mother, and I couldn't be trusted to care.

By chance one day, an errand in town left me with hours to kill. Before I could think about it too much, I climbed the concrete stairs and made my way to the secure library. The archivist handed me a sheet of instructions and made me sign a paper that informed me of my liability in handling the director's journals. I could be prosecuted if I caused any damage. She had me put on a pair of white cotton gloves, intended to keep the oils and perspiration of my hands from harming the fragile materials. Then she wheeled a cart inside the locked archive room, put down a flat box containing several years' worth of journals on it, and left the cart and box next to me, telling me I'd have until the library closed to review them.

I read the director's notes from the day Mother was committed, trying to conjure my mother from the page by absorbing fully what was there, and what wasn't. I wasn't sure how long my courage would hold out. Waves of nausea came and went, my hands trembled, and my breathing was shallow and fast. I rubbed my eyes and sat back in the chair, willing myself to slow down. I'd made it inside and didn't necessarily need to hurry through, but I couldn't completely squelch my fear that I'd learn too much or too little. So be it, I told myself. If I had to, I would define her by all the empty space around her as if I were snipping a sheet of black paper to create a silhouette. In which case, I'd need to pay even more attention to what I could learn. I took several deep breaths and went on.

The director carefully recorded that on Mother's commitment day the temperature outside was below zero, the snow was up to the first-floor windowsills, and one unfortunate patient was found frozen to death on the grounds. While the height of the snow made for an attractively higher landing spot for that inmate's escape plan, the frigid temperatures put an end to it. The director wrote the weather report and its impact on the escapee on the bottom of the page under the heading "Discharged/Deceased."

Under "Admissions" he had written her name only, adding the description in the margins, making me question the truth of what was written even more. Was he factually describing her or someone else? Why were these details marginalized, while the weather got prominent notice on the page? Was the weather more deserving of his thoughts than she was?

"Albumen skin" seemed insulting, as if he were describing a broken egg and not a person. The phrase sounded like the words from an autopsy. His prognosis was that she was destined never to leave the place alive.

My adoptive mother's words came to me again.

Still, the director had been struck enough by her to make a hurried note in the margin. Nowhere else in the journal had I seen anything like what he wrote. The rest of the writing was kept within the margins and there were no other physical descriptions of any other arriving inmates. It had to be about her, I was convinced. People could describe me in the same way, especially if they were feeling less than charitable. All my life I'd wondered if I resembled her. At last, I knew I did.

I spent a few more hours combing through his other journals up until the date corresponding with census records I'd already researched from the era. She hadn't been listed in the census taken a few years after my birth and her incarceration. I'd made sure to read the pages of inmates' names not once but twice. Forty pages of men and women who were at the asylum the date of the census and not a trace of her. I'd hoped that meant she had left town after being released from the asylum and went on to a fulfilling life elsewhere. But there was no record of her in the Discharged/Deceased section of his log either. She had been admitted, then disappeared, whited out the moment she stepped within.

I glanced at the clock and saw that my time was nearly up, several hours quickly elapsing as I paged through the journals. There was nothing more to learn about her except that she was tiny and thin, with yolk-colored hair and albumen skin.

She would never be more than an absence from my life. She would always be defined by the negative space that enveloped her. I quietly slipped off one of the gloves, kissed my finger, and ran it across the words, leaving a trace of myself on the one portrait I had of her—an asylum director's notation in the margins.

Gift Wrapped

"This is heaven?" Melody asked upon seeing the boring brick building on Rice Street. The man standing at the door did not look like an angel, unless angels smoked cigars and had huge bellies that suspenders could barely support. The cigar-smoking angel did not answer her question, and her mother was still hurrying to catch up with Melody, who had skipped ahead.

Melody's mother had told her that they would have lunch soon after they arrived to see Poppa, whom Melody had been told had gone to heaven. It was both confusing and wonderful—to see Poppa, visit heaven, and have lunch there, all in one day.

"You understand, don't you?" her mother had asked. "It's a visitation. A celebration of Grandpa's life."

"A party?"

"In some ways. Yes."

Naturally, Melody wondered next whether cake was served inside heaven. She hoped it wasn't like the kind Kara had at her birthday. Carrot cake. Yuck. The frosting had been yummy, and Melody had licked hers clean, then helped herself to Kara's little brother's frosting, too. The cake at her cousin's party had been much better—chocolate with chocolate frosting. She'd had a hundred pieces.

"Mama," she asked when her mother caught up to her. "What kind of cake will they have at Grandpa's party?"

"Cake?" Her mother stroked Melody's hair. "Well, I suppose there might be cake."

Her mother wasn't sure there'd be cake? What kind of party could you have without cake?

They passed by the potbellied angel and stepped inside, walking through a thickly carpeted hallway that Melody longed to run through but couldn't since her mother held her hand so tightly. People whispered. Some cried quietly.

There wasn't a balloon or present to be seen. Poppa's visitation didn't seem much like a party at all, she wanted to complain. But the hushed atmosphere made her timid and her mother's grip was growing more commanding by the moment.

When they came to a small side room, Melody saw a table full of party treats including small pieces of lemon cake on little plates. Melody's mother finally let her go and Melody helped herself to several slices, a few handsful of nuts, several cookies, and several glasses of punch.

She spotted her grandpa lying in an ornate box at the far end of the adjacent room, surrounded by an entire flower shop's worth of arrangements. The box Poppa slept in was lined with purple silk the color of Melody's favorite party dress. Melody watched as people approached him, said a few words, wiped their noses, then walked away.

Finally, when Grandpa was alone and Melody was full of party treats, she approached him. She kissed his cool cheek, just as she had seen others do, and was surprised by the rigid feel of it. But most perplexing were his glasses, perched unnecessarily atop his nose, positioned squarely in front of his closed eyes.

Melody felt a question forming in her mind and turned to look for her mother, but her mother was at the opposite side of the room and in a conversation with strangers. Besides, what would she ask, exactly?

Melody would simply have to find out for herself. She stood on her tiptoes, and with a sharp twist of her shoulders, she was able to lay her head on the pillow next to his.

She looked out through Poppa's glasses, imagining the view he saw in heaven and whispering to him about one he couldn't see. "The cake was delicious, Poppa," she said. "Best I ever tasted."

Stranger at the Bad Luck Ball

On the moonless winter evening of January 13, 1922, Cliff Aron was tending bar at St. Paul's University Club, having been hired by F. Scott and Zelda Fitzgerald for their "Bad Luck Ball." Cliff was Scott's favorite bartender from the nearby Commodore Hotel where the Fitzgeralds were regulars. They currently resided in a house a few blocks away at 626 Goodrich, and Zelda disliked the place intensely. "Much too boring," she'd said to Scott when they drank at the Commodore.

"She's been in a terrible mood for months now," Scott told Cliff. "I'm hoping the ball will cheer her up." Now that Fitzgerald's books and short stories were selling well, he had the means to keep Zelda richly entertained.

Zelda's high spirits were on ample display that night from the moment she entered the Club and dropped off her coat to an attendant in the ladies' cloak room. She'd hurried to the bar for the first of many gin

& juices, her favorite. Cliff had drinks waiting for both Fitzgeralds, but from the smell of alcohol already on her breath, the slur in her southern-accented voice and her brightly flushed cheeks, it was clear that this was not her first drink of the evening. "I am absolutely giddy to be here," she said before dancing away in the elite, recently opened Club.

Located on Summit Avenue at the top of Ramsey Hill, the University Club was an instant favorite of the wealthy, all of whom quickly snapped up memberships the day it opened in 1913. In-demand St. Paul architects—Reed and Stern—had designed the Tudor-style building inspired by similar clubs in England, New York and elsewhere. They'd also designed Grand Central Station in New York City and numerous other St. Paul buildings and mansions along Summit Avenue, validating who belonged to the upper class. The Fitzgeralds didn't, and Cliff knew Scott resented that.

Zelda's loud laugh regularly punctuated the sound of the jaunty jazz band hired for the evening. Many flocked to be near to her. The women wore risqué, shimmering, short dresses. Their lumber and rail baron, banker, and political husbands drank and danced wildly with their wives, sometimes with other men's wives. Bootlegged liquor flowed freely into the glamorous crowd, keeping Cliff busy at the bar. Cliff knew none of these leading citizens of St. Paul feared arrest.

* * *

Cliff had a moment to look around the room once most of the guests were already drinking their third or fourth cocktail of the night. Cliff recognized everybody there because they all frequented the Commodore, but one guest, an elegantly dressed young woman who couldn't have been more than twenty, was a stranger to him.

She seemed to have no husband or date at her side, but there were other single people at the ball, and he saw her dancing a few times with eligible sons of well-known couples. Her blond hair was fashionably cropped into a bob and a diamond studded headband sparkled in the gentle finger waves she'd styled. Strands of pearls dripped from her earrings and brushed against her neck. The stranger's black dress seemed slightly plain next to the lavishly beaded creations worn by other wealthy women in the room, but it was just as short. A length of shiny black fringe glistened from the dress's hem as she danced, and an elaborate, diamond studded choker and two very fine silver bracelets sparkled with her slightest movement.

She *looked* like she fit in, but he was certain she didn't belong there. He knew Zelda and Scott didn't belong there either. They were not at all wealthy and did not have the necessary pedigree. They'd been evicted from their rental home in Dellwood and spent a month at the Commodore before moving to the boring St. Paul house. But St. Paul's elite were happy to have them in town, even though Scott made fun of them in his satirical newspaper, *The St. Paul Daily Dirge, Mortuary Edition*. Everyone had received the latest copy written for the occasion as they entered the University Club.

The young stranger caught Cliff looking at her and made her way to the bar without hesitation. She ordered a gin and juice—expertly requesting a double—and sat at the bar to drink it. A copy of the Fitzgeralds' fake newspaper had been left there by a guest. Cliff saw she had no copy of her own, unless she had already tucked it into the beautifully sequined clutch she laid on the bar.

As she sipped her drink, her eyes were on the big bold headline: "COTILLION IS SAD FAILURE!" Cliff saw her trail a finger slowly down the left column story, "Frightful Orgy at University Club," reading aloud Fitzgerald's description of "these vain frivolous peacocks who strut through the gorgeous vistas of the exclusive and corrupt St. Paul clubs…"

"Did he write about you?" Cliff rakishly asked, hoping to find out who she was.

She raised her eyes to his, gave him a half smile, then answered him in a challenging yet silky voice that told him she was flirting back.

"Do you think he did?" She nodded to her empty glass and he quickly refilled it. He had no idea how to answer her.

* * *

The hosts moved close to the bar, and Scott said, "Cliff, give us two of what she's having."

Cliff quickly complied, pouring doubles for both Fitzgeralds while keeping an eye on his bar.

Zelda frowned at the girl Scott had pointed out. "I haven't seen this one before," she snapped at him. Cliff had seen Zelda ignite into a rage, even on the happiest of occasions, souring the moment she sensed a slight. "That young woman may be rich," Zelda erupted, seeing the jewels sparkling on the unknown woman's neck and wrists, "but she's the plainest thing I ever saw!"

The entire room hushed. Many had witnessed both the highs and the lows the Fitzgeralds brought into any room they visited, the countless times they'd been asked to leave after causing disruptions. Everyone knew they were witnessing firsthand an example of the bad behavior that resulted in the Fitzgeralds' evictions from more than one fine hotel.

"She's nothing compared to you," a handsome son of the town's wealthiest banker said to Zelda.

"Silly, it's true!" Scott immediately added. "Let's dance!"

Zelda snorted and giggled and followed Scott onto the dance floor. But instead of taking his hand, she beckoned to the young man who'd complimented her, her good spirits quickly returning. The guests roared and clapped in their moment of payback for Scott's rude stories about them in the *Daily Dirge*.

* * *

Cliff chuckled and turned his attention back to the mysterious woman, but she'd left the bar. He scanned the room for signs of her for the rest of the night, but never saw her and he couldn't leave his post. The last guest left the University Club at three in the morning, and as Cliff was closing the bar, the woman's cloak room attendant brought a small box to him.

"I can't believe how careless women are with their expensive things," the woman said. Cliff couldn't place the voice, though he thought he'd heard one like it at some point during the ball. "Will you arrange to have these lost and found items locked in the safe until someone has the sense to claim them?"

The young woman wore a heavy wool coat, a gray wool-felt cloche, and plain wool gloves. A few blond waves slipped out of the cloche. Her face was clean of the heavy makeup all the rest of the ladies had worn that evening, but he noticed a slight flush in her cheeks, the remnants of coloring in her lips.

He took the box from her as she gave him a half smile.

"Good night for tips," she commented, shaking her simple handbag. "You too?"

He nodded. Cliff thought he remembered the smile, the silken challenge of her voice. She said nothing more than good night, then exited the University Club's front door.

Cliff examined the contents of the box and immediately recognized the beautifully sequined clutch, the hair band, the pearl earrings, the diamond studded choker, and the two very fine silver bracelets.

He hurried to the door to try and catch the ladies' cloak room attendant—the stranger he now knew was the mystery woman at the bar, the one who'd caught both his and the Fitzgeralds' notice—but she was gone by then in the moonless early morning hours of January 14th.

Playing House

Millicent walked—or rather, hopped—with a notice-able limp. Before she headed out the door forever, she wanted to make sure her pink chiffon dress strategical-ly hid her missing leg. As she was slightly tippy, she leaned on the doorframe, gazing through the acetate window as she adjusted her crinoline.

"Millicent," Reginald said in alarm, his voice both high-pitched and manly, "you're leaving me? Without a word?"

Reginald's skull fracture had healed nicely, but little globs of white glue marred his perfect black hel-met of hair. A piece of his skull had never been found—"a war injury," Reginald always pointed out—and the skull was repaired askew, leaving him with a jagged but heroic-looking scar across his missing eye.

"Yes," Millicent said a bit too dramatically. She composed herself, and said something she knew she would probably regret.

"Why, of course, you idiot!"

She did regret those words, because they were far too blasé when the situation called for hysterics.

She threw herself onto the rosewood settee, the one where Janey had laid her lime-green lollypop. The lollypop stuck to Millicent's best—and only—dress, its gloppy syrup instantly gluing her to the settee. She was stuck, and that was the last thing she wanted Reginald to know.

She calmly smoothed her dress, once again strategically positioning it over her missing leg. She casually leaned one stiff arm on the settee, thinking her blurry reflection in the tinfoil mirror quite handsome.

"What shall I tell the children?" Reginald whispered in a quavering voice, his glass eye shining with unshed tears.

Six-year-old Maisie quietly played inside of the closed refrigerator, while the babies, Max and Mitzi, sat unattended in the bathtub on the second floor, unaware of the drama unfolding between their parents.

Frederick, the toddler, dangled on the outside of the house, clinging to the attic windowsill with his one good hand.

"I don't have the foggiest clue, Reginald," Janey said in disgusted tones for Millicent. "You're on your own."

Suddenly, rumbling sounded from beyond the kitchen window. A moment later, the entire house began to shake, the fine bone china flying out of the balsa wood buffet, the pantry springing open and strewing its contents everywhere.

Frederick fell from the window. Maisie's refrigerator tumbled off the roof. The tub capsized, spilling the twins onto the bedroom floor.

Reginald and Millicent were thrown into an awkward and not terribly passionate embrace.

A ferocious beast snapped up Max and Mitzi and ran out of the room, spurring Janey into action.

"Nugget!" she shouted as her beagle ran away with the babies in his jaws. Nugget disappeared through the dog door, and Janey scrambled through, close behind.

She knew exactly where he was headed. The raspberry bushes.

"Nugget! Stop!"

It was too late. Nugget dove under the scratchy raspberry bushes and Janey steeled herself. She crept in, the thorns pricking her skinny arms and poking her face. She dragged the dog out by his collar, grabbed his skull and shook the twins loose.

They were a slobbery mess, but still intact. Mitzi had new chew marks on her tiny arm. Max's head wasn't any worse than it was the last time Nugget ran off with him.

Janey returned triumphantly to her bedroom, one plastic baby in each hand. Reginald and Millicent were still clinging to each other, their dollhouse in shambles.

Janey licked her lollypop free of the settee and set off to find the white glue.

Elephant in the Room

One day, Darby and Marcella were quietly having lunch outside the office where they both worked. Like always, Darby was having Braunschweiger with mustard on wheat and Marcella was having a jelly sandwich on white. Marcella had just unwrapped her jelly sandwich when Darby popped his question.

"What's the difference between an elephant and a flea?"

Marcella opened the small spiral notebook she brought every day to lunch, and began to write the question down, but then paused. She removed another notebook from her purse and flipped through it rapidly.

"Ah ha," she announced. "October 14th."

"You're sure about that?"

"An elephant can have fleas, but a flea can't have elephants." She snapped the notebook shut.

"Noooo!" he moaned. "You have to give me another chance. According to the rules, right?"

Marcella located another notebook, even more ragged than the one she'd just shut. "After the first joke repetition, Darby is allowed to tell another elephant joke. If he repeats himself with the second joke, he has one last question."

Darby thought long and hard. Marcella took a bite of her sandwich.

The elephant jokes had begun a few years earlier, when Darby came across Marcella during the noon hour. She was sitting exactly where she was now, quietly crying into her jelly sandwich.

They'd been acquaintances, but not yet friends, and that day she needed a friend. She told him she'd just been dumped by her fiancé, a junior executive in the marketing division. Darby handed her a tissue and offered to marry her on the spot.

He was more serious than she knew but made the offer sound like a joke. She sniffled that he must be joking but thanked him anyway. It was then he told the first elephant joke.

She laughed harder than she'd ever laughed at anything. Well now, she said. He was welcome to join her for lunch any day, as long as the elephant jokes held out. There were literally trunks of elephant jokes, he quipped, so she wouldn't be rid of him any time soon.

Now it seemed he had finally run out of material. Mustard dripped from his sandwich onto his shirt. Finally, one came to him. "How can you tell whether you're eating elephant or peanut butter?"

"Elephant doesn't stick to the roof of your mouth!" she said triumphantly without referencing her notes.

Darby gasped and turned pale. "I have one final shot. Right?"

"Right. You remember what happens if the jokes run out?" Marcella dabbed at Darby's mustard stain.

Yes. He knew. It would be time to get serious. Her broken heart had long since healed, yet he was the one dragging his feet, unwilling to take a risk.

All he'd ever asked of her was one more day, one more lunch, another new joke. Why get serious? Wouldn't that end it for them? Still, he'd agreed to the rules.

He'd told all the elephant in the refrigerator jokes, all the jokes about how many elephants you can fit in taxis and Volkswagens. Why elephants have blue shoes (white shoes get dirty too fast), why they float upside down (to keep their blue shoes dry), all the jokes about elephants crossing the road, with and without chickens. All the wordplay jokes—elephones (how elephants communicate), elecoptors (what's big and grey and can fly straight up?), elevision (what elephants do for entertainment).

There was only one question left.

Darby got down on his knees and held Marcella's hand. "I'm out of elephant jokes. Will you marry me anyway?"

Happy tears accompanied her answer.
Yes!

Whole Lotta Bull

Mendota County Detective Arvo Thorson finished his second Pronto Pup shortly before he arrived at the murder scene. He elbowed his way through the crowd gathered outside the Creative Activities building, his notebook in hand and a suitably grim look on his face.

He hoped no one would notice that his shirt was stained with the telltale sign of French's yellow mustard.

The Minnesota State Fair was in full swing and at nine o'clock on a hot, late August Tuesday, thousands of potential suspects could have already come and gone through the clacking turnstiles. The perpetrator could easily be miles away already. Any delay, even for a mouthwatering Pronto Pup or two, would be inexcusable.

Except that in this case, the apparent murderer had already been shot dead by the Falcon Heights police. The press had already opened and shut this sensational case in the space of three hours, as was neatly summarized by a morning DJ.

"Rampaging Bull Gores Pie Contest Judge! That's right, you heard it here first on F-A-I-R RADIO!"

The press had gotten ahead of the facts as usual, thought Thorson. And at the moment, there were only three facts as Detective Thorson duly noted in his dime-store notebook:

1. Betty Bruckle, the State Fair pie judge, was dead, with a gaping stab wound in her chest. Her body was slumped next to the prize jam and jelly case.

2. A 1500-pound Black angus bull had been shot dead by the local police department. It lay in a heap twenty feet away from the dead judge, a display of lacy doilies and antimacassars nearby.

3. The blue-ribbon strawberry rhubarb pie baked by Barbie Bruckle, the judge's sister-in-law, was missing.

A teary young boy wearing an FFA shirt sat next to the bull's carcass, his arm around the black beast's neck, his hand softly caressing the massive forehead.

"This your bull, young man?" Thorson asked softly.

The slight, freckled boy who couldn't be more than twelve or thirteen nodded. It seemed impossible that the huge bull belonged to this fragile young lad. Yet the animal had obviously been much fussed over. Its black coat was shiny as obsidian, smoothed clean of loose hairs, and its hooves manicured far better than Thorson's stubby, chewed nails would ever be.

The boy protectively cradled the dead bull's head in his lap, his fingers absently massaging the bull's velvety ears.

"I… don't understand. Cuddles… wouldn't hurt nobody." The boy dragged his forearm under his snotty nose.

"Cuddles. That's the bull's name?"

"Yes sir, it is."

"What's your name, son?" Thorson asked.

"Lyle. Johnson."

The boy announced his name with the force of a slap. Clearly, he was growing angrier by the moment. "I raised Cuddles from a runt calf. I know him like he was my own flesh and blood. He wouldn't hurt nobody, no sir."

"Do you have any idea how he got here, all the way across the fairgrounds?"

"No. I got to his pen at six a.m. and the door was wide open. I ran down every street calling for him. When I heard the gun shots in the distance, I couldn't believe what I was hearing."

The boy glanced at the dead bull and then looked back at Thorson with a resolute and certain expression in his baby blues. By Thorson's estimation, the boy suddenly matured a good four or five years in the space of thirty seconds.

"He didn't kill that lady, no sir. He's been framed, isn't that what they call it? I'm an honest kid and I know Cuddles through and through. He didn't murder no one."

Thorson realized something was missing from the bull. He leaned in and whispered something in the boy's ears.

"No sir. They never do," the boy answered.

Thorson patted the boy on the shoulder and thanked him.

One of the Falcon Heights cops motioned to Thorson.

"Bill, isn't it?" Thorson asked with his hand out.

"That's right, you've got a good memory. We haven't seen you out here for ten years, is it? That was the year the Department had a booth in the Grandstand. You were here with your beautiful wife. I remember how your missus laughed when she tried the Breathalyzer. How is that lovely lady?"

Thorson flinched and hoped Bill hadn't noticed. The divorce had only become final in the past few months. Helen had wanted out for pretty much all those ten years and when he finally gave in, she quickly moved on, letting it slip that the next weekend she'd gone out on her first post-divorce date with the same man she'd been seeing on the side for a decade. Apparently, the gossip hadn't made its way to Falcon Heights yet.

He was still in love with her. No one knew why, least of all Thorson.

"She's fine," Thorson said quickly. "You know something about this witness?"

"Yeah, some carny by the name of MacGregor."

Thorson flipped open his notebook and jotted down the name.

"What's his story?"

"He's new at the Fair this year. Mechanic at the fun house. He's from down south, Louisiana or Oklahoma."

"Aren't they all …"

"You bet."

Thorson underlined Louisiana and Oklahoma. His stomach growled. He wondered whether there was a Tom Thumb mini donuts stand nearby.

"Only thing we have is this carny saying he stepped into a stinking fresh pile of bull manure sometime past five-thirty a.m. as he was walking into St. Urho's Dining Hall. They have him over there now waiting for you, though I don't know why. It's pretty clear the bull wandered over here, passed St. Urho's, got in here and gored that poor lady."

"I'm not so sure the bull did it. I mean look at the size of him. I would have expected to see more blood-stained hoof prints, more signs of a struggle, more damage to these display cases. I mean, that's a lot of bull, Bill, and this place is practically a China shop. And you seemed to have missed a significant bit of evidence here."

"What's that, Detective?"

Thorson looked at the tear-stained boy again. "That bull hasn't got any horns. That's why they call Angus 'polled.' They never have any horns."

"Oh," the cop said, embarrassed.

Thorson kneeled next to Lyle again and put a hand on the boy's shoulder. "I'm sorry, son. I've got some work to do now." He handed the boy his card. "If you notice or hear anything else, I want you to call me."

Thorson headed out to see MacGregor at the Dining Hall. The weather was fine, sunny and still. The thick, heavy air smelled of all manner of dipped and fried things—cheese curds, onion blossoms, candy bars and chocolate wrapped bacon. Under the sweet and oily smells, there was another pungent one. Body odor. It was going to be a hot one.

Thorson walked down Cosgrove and sure enough, there was a mini-donut booth right at the Dan Patch intersection. He traded a couple of dollars for a hot, greasy, sugary bag of mini donuts, consuming them in a flash and licking his fingers clean. He'd get some coffee at St. Urho's.

His cell phone buzzed. It was Helen texting him, "U R late again!"

He cursed when he remembered. The alimony check. He texted back. "Sorry. Tonight."

He arrived in front of St. Urho's Dining Hall and ritualistically touched the chain saw sculpture of the legendary Finn, said to have cast frogs out of Finland by his loud voice. Legend had it that Urho loved sour milk and fish soup, both of which were prominently featured on the Dining Hall's menu though they were seldom ordered. Thorson's mother had been Finnish, his father Swedish, a mixed marriage according to Minnesota Scandinavian immigrant standards.

The carny was sitting in a dark booth in the back hunched over a plate of pie. When Thorson sat down across from him, the man cowered. He seemed nervous. Too nervous.

A waitress walked over with Thorson's cup of coffee.

"You want some coffee?" Thorson asked the carny.

The carny nodded and smiled slightly, revealing a mouth full of broken and missing teeth. Thorson was starting to prefer the cowering version. He didn't want to see those teeth.

The basic information had already been taken down by the local police, one of whom was standing nearby. Thorson scanned through the carny's demographics. Ferdinand MacGregor. Birthplace: Baton Rouge. Age: forty-six or forty-seven, he's not sure. Permanent address: none.

"You go by Ferdinand?"

"People call me Nando."

"Umm. Okay, Nando. So why don't you tell me what happened this morning."

Nando casually speared a forkful of pie from what remained on his plate as he relayed a story that was not too different from what Bill had already told him.

"You said you came here around five in the morning?

"Around then. It was early."

"Sun up then?"

"Yeah. Sure. The sun was up." Nando dragged his finger across his plate, dabbing up the bright red sticky juice.

"Seems to me that it might have been later than five a.m.," Thorson suggested. "When I drove in to work this morning at six-thirty, it was still dark. Are you sure the sun was up when you got here?"

"When I got here," Nando sucked on his finger. "Now, you may be right about that sir. Maybe it was later. Yes. You're right. I think it was more like seven-thirty."

"So, it was seven-thirty. You arrive at St. Urho's. You're walking up to the front door. Then what happens."

"I stepped right into that bull s___, I mean dung. I stepped into it."

"Tell me more about that. Do you remember whether it seemed like it was fresh or not? Had it been there awhile?"

"Well, it sure seemed fresh to me. I don't know much about cows. Alligators, that's more what I know." He threw his head back and laughed.

Thorson looked away to avoid the sight of the teeth. "Do you remember whether it seemed hot? Or cold? Solid or not much?"

"I can't really remember all of that. I know I had to clean off my boots before I came in here."

Nando picked up his plate and gave it a final lick.

"That must have been some pie," Thorson said. "What was it? Strawberry rhubarb?"

"Yes, it was."

"I think I might order some myself." Thorson had already made note of St. Urho's menu. No pie of any kind. Ever. He'd been coming to St. Urho's for years and had never seen pie on the menu.

The cowering expression returned. "I think they're out for today."

Thorson called the cop over.

"Mr. Nando, would you mind showing me what you have in that bag on your lap?"

"Umm…" Nando was trying to think fast, Thorson could see it in his eyes. "Well, sure. Why not?" He handed the bag to Thorson.

Thorson opened it and saw a half-eaten pie. He lifted the pie pan slowly out of the bag. The filling was a fire-red mixture of fibrous rhubarb and chunky strawberries. A blue-ribbon dangled beneath it.

"Hmm. No wonder it's good. It won the blue-ribbon. Seems to have been baked by a B. Bruckle."

The carny replied, "I don't know anything about that officer. Some guy gave it to me this morning. He just ran by and handed it to me. I don't know anything else but that."

Something else was stuck to the bottom of the pie pan. It was a ticket stub with writing on it, stained red with strawberry-rhubarb sauce.

"I think you'll need to head down to the station for more questioning, Mr. MacGregor. A lot more questioning. At the moment, you're looking more like an accessory to a murder, possibly the prime suspect, unless you have a better explanation for how you and this pie came together this morning."

That was enough for the cork to come out of Nando. A skinny, middle-aged man had stopped him late the previous night with a strange request and a hundred-dollar bill. First thing in the morning, Nando was to bring some fresh manure from the cattle pens over to St. Urho's and dump it out front. If anyone asked, he was to tell the story of having come upon it in the wee hours of the morning and stepped into it when it was fresh. The man dropped by St. Urho's this morning and nodded at Nando, handing him the bag with the pie and another hundred dollars for his troubles. Nando knew enough to not ask many questions about this kind of assignment.

"You need to be available for more questioning," Thorson said. "Don't even consider leaving the fairgrounds until we've told you. Do you understand?"

"Yes sir."

Nando got up to leave. "I suppose I can't have the rest of that pie."

"You are correct."

Thorson's phone buzzed again. It was another text from his ex. "Where R U?"

He responded, typing slowly with his thick fingers. "Fair. On a case."

Her response was instant. "Will meet U in 60."

His phone rang before he could respond.

"Detective, it's Bill. They said you should head over to the cattle barns. Crime scene investigators found something in Cuddle's pen."

"Tell them I'm on my way."

Thorson left St. Urho's and walked down Cosgrove, taking a shortcut behind the band shell and then a quick detour through the food building. After that last text from his ex-wife, he knew he needed more Fair food. He'd gained a good fifteen pounds since the divorce and planned to slim down soon. After the Fair. Until then, he'd eat well, hoping the food would absorb the acid that had built up over the past year.

He handed a couple of dollars to a girl wearing a foam cheese-wedge hat and in turn received a greasy basket of hot, fried cheese curds. He ate them too soon and burned his tongue, but he knew he'd have to gobble them down quick as he trotted down Carnes Avenue. He almost stopped for a Reuben sandwich at Schumacher's but knew that would take too long.

He turned south on Nelson, cutting through the DNR area and glancing quickly in the fishpond. In the shady depths, prehistoric looking gars and gigantic muskellunge floated silently. Nearer to the surface, rainbow trout flitted through the dappled sunlight. The water looked cool, and Thorson found himself wishing he was floating in there with them.

He looked ahead and saw his next stop, the all-you-can-drink milk booth. The cheese curds had been delicious but salty. Thorson paid a dollar and drank down three quick cups, finishing a fourth while he continued along Judson to the cattle barn. He wondered again, as he had when he had first spoke to Lyle, how Cuddles could have made it all the way through the fair without anyone noticing.

He saw the crime scene tape around a pen near the entrance to the cattle barn. Posted outside the pen was a picture of Lyle and Cuddles in better times.

"I heard you found something here?" Thorson asked.

A crime scene investigator with plastic gloves held up a clear plastic bag containing a bloody metal pie spatula.

"Ah. The real murder weapon?"

"We'll have to test to be sure, but we are fairly certain that is not strawberry-rhubarb dripping from the edge. It was buried in the corner here under some hay. In a Fleet Farm bag."

Thorson remembered the ticket stub and fished it out of his pocket. He could just make out the writing on the back of the stub. It was a phone number. He jotted it into his notebook before handing the stub to the crime scene investigator.

He dialed the number on his cell phone.

"State Fair Security," said the voice on the other end of the line.

Interesting, Thorson thought as he announced himself. He asked for a log of all the calls in the past twenty-four hours. "Were you on duty this morning?"

"Yep. We got that call around seven-thirty this morning. The one about a bull in the Creative Activities building."

"What time does the building open?"

"That's the stumper. The building doesn't even open until eight a.m."

"Does Security monitor the building before it opens?"

"No. We're not sure how a person could have been in there yet, let alone a bull. They found a broken lock on one of the Education building doors.

"That's next to Creative Activities, right?"

"Yep. They're connected."

"Get the caller's name?"

"No, but we'll have the caller's phone number on the log. Possibly a name."

"You're in the admin building? Right across from Creative Activities on Dan Patch?"

"That's right, Detective. We'll get the log ready for you."

"Appreciate it. See you in about fifteen minutes."

Thorson had already planned his route back to the crime scene. A brisk walk north on Liggett would take him right past the Midway and to the Grandstand. On his way, he saw Nando just outside the funhouse with his bag of tools. He wondered if Nando had hidden the pie spatula in Cuddles' pen. Thorson motioned him over.

"Take a walk with me."

Nando smiled nervously, revealing his nasty-looking teeth. "Sure," he said, "No problem." The detective and the carny turned at Carnes.

"Do you mind if we make a quick stop?" Thorson asked as they neared the corn on the cob booth. "Want some?"

"No, thank you, detective. Gives me gas." Another nervous smile.

Thorson methodically began eating the corn. "Mind if I ask a few more questions?"

"No problem."

"This guy meets you this morning at St. Urho's before eight a.m.?"

"Right. After sunrise."

"You said he handed you the pie and some money?"

"That's right."

"What else can you tell me about him?

"He was dressed nice, that I can tell you. He had a blue suit and tie. Seemed like some kind of a businessman."

"A businessman?"

"He had a cell phone clipped to his belt and he was wearing one of those fancy earpieces. He was talking on the cell phone when he got here. He was carrying a lot of stuff. I think that's why he unloaded the pie on me."

"What else was he carrying?"

"He had a lot of rope and a big grocery bag that looked like it had some clothes in it. And he had another bag—I think it was a Fleet Farm bag. Kind of strange a businessman with a Fleet Farm bag and a lot of rope."

Thorson finished his corn. A couple of girls dressed in old country costumes got Nando's attention. They wore sashes reading "Slovakian Dancers." Both girls were sturdy-looking blond farm girls.

Nando nodded as they approached the corn stand. "Where are you ladies from?" he asked, sensibly keeping his teeth covered.

"Wadena!" one shrieked.

Her dairy-girl twin slapped her. "Joanie, don't be talking to strangers."

"Want some free Midway passes?" Nando offered. "Got a one-eyed friend called Pirate Jack that runs the bottle cap game in the Midway. Go see him and tell him Nando sent you. You'll win the biggest animal he's got."

"See, Patsy?" the giggler shrieked to her friend. "He's nicer than he looks."

"Joanie!" Patsy said, slapping her friend again. "Our dads will give us hell for talking to this guy."

"I don't care," Joanie said, pertly accepting the tickets.

"Stop by the funhouse, that's where I work. I'll find some more passes for you girls. Girls all the way from Wadena should have a good time at the Midway, I'll see to it." Nando winked and smiled at both girls.

"We definitely won't be seeing you," Patsy said as she took her cob and left.

"I'm not so sure about that," Joanie said, smiling at the ugly carny.

Thorson couldn't believe this murder suspect was such a flirt, as ugly as he was. But stranger things had happened today.

"Those girls were nice. What's Wadena anyway?" the carny drawled, watching the girls sashay away.

"It's a small town in northwestern Minnesota. Say, do you mind coming along with me? I'm thinking you might remember more if you saw the crime scene."

"Why sure!" Nando said enthusiastically.

Thorson was sure that Nando wasn't smart enough to fake that level of excitement. He was acting like a little kid who'd been allowed to stay up past his bedtime. A little kid with bad teeth and the hots for some farm girls.

A few minutes later, Thorson and Nando had made it to the State Fair Security building and Thorson had a copy of the call log in his hands. "Three calls between seven a.m. and eight a.m. This one here is from the call about the bull being in Creative Activities. It's a local area code. They even have a name. Crosby. Looks like another lead to follow up."

"Does that name mean anything to you? Crosby?" Thorson asked.

"No." Nando scratched his chin, screwing up his forehead as he appeared to honestly try to recollect anything else. "You detectives sure have to put a lot together."

"Let's go to the Creative Activities building. I want to look things over again."

"I'll look things over too. Maybe something else will come back to me."

Nando lifted his shoulders and kept up with Thorson, more energy in his step than Thorson had seen in him today. He'd gained a sidekick. Every cop needs his sidekick. But a carny with bad teeth? Thorson and Nando. He was hoping for someone more like Tonto or Robin.

Thorson's phone buzzed again. "My ex-wife," he explained to Nando.

"Ex-wife. I got a couple of those myself. What's she want?"

"She's here at the Fair. Come to collect her alimony." He texted his location in reply.

"Now you know why I got no permanent address."

Thorson smiled at Nando for the first time that day. "I'll have to consider that myself."

They arrived at the Creative Activities building entrance. The place was packed with fairgoers looking at display cases of hand-made crafts, quilts, clothing, lamps, rugs, and toys. An elaborately gaudy bald eagle carving attracted Nando.

"Wouldn't you love that hanging over your fireplace?" Nando gushed, genuinely impressed.

Not really, Thorson thought. He was living in a tiny, cramped apartment. No fireplace, not that he'd want a bald eagle hanging over it if he had one.

Thorson led Nando through the handicraft displays all the way back to the food section. The crime-scene tape had been removed, along with the dead bodies. Ahead of them, Thorson saw Lyle Johnson.

"They carted Cuddles out back and loaded him on a trailer. They're going to take him over to the Ag school and cremate him. I couldn't stand to see that."

"Nando, this is Lyle. He raised the bull they shot for no reason at all."

"Sorry to hear that, Lyle. I'm sure he was a fine bull."

"Thank you, Mr. Nando."

State Fair officials had gathered near the pie display cases and were removing the pies.

"I heard somebody say they have to do the pie judging over since that winning pie was stolen."

The substitute judge was a thin, bald man with a knobby Adam's apple and an intense expression. He wore a blue suit and pinned to his lapel was an official nametag with the State Fair logo on it. He had a cell phone clipped to his belt and an earpiece.

Next to him stood a thick-set, middle-aged woman who wore large, round, white-rimmed sunglasses and dark lipstick. She was nearly hairless herself. She smiled primly, clutching a badly made knock-off purse.

The man held up a new blue-ribbon for the gathered audience to see and placed it on the thick-set woman's pie. Thorson inched close to the judge, close enough to read the name on his name tag.

"Crosby."

Behind Thorson, two familiar voices spoke, one after the other.

First, Nando announced too loudly "Hey, that's the guy. That's the guy that gave me the money and the pie. He's the guy who told me to put the manure at St. Urho's."

Then Thorson heard his ex-wife's voice. "Arvo Thorson! I want my money. Now!"

Thorson backed up slightly and turned. Some-thing flew by his face. Strangely, his ex-wife's face was suddenly covered with pie. The crowd gasped and Thorson swiveled back around to see the judge aiming another pie at him point blank.

Suddenly it was the side of the judge's face that was covered in pie. The side that faced Nando, who smiled a victorious, gap-toothed grin at everyone pres-ent. The crowd booed.

Pies began to fly everywhere aimed in particular at the dirty carny who ducked for cover behind a dis-play case of nut breads. Thorson stepped toward Cros-by, who was trying to steal away across the slippery, pie-covered floor. A chocolate cream pie flew onto the fat woman's head, the chocolate shavings creating the hairpiece she was sorely missing. A trio of lime pies creamed a set of elderly Swiss triplets. A middle-aged father took advantage of the mayhem and pushed his pouty teen daughter's face into a meringue.

Lyle attempted to run around the jam and jelly case and cut off Crosby. Instead, Crosby grabbed the boy and a pie spatula, aiming the pointed end at the boy's neck.

"Everyone, back off or the boy gets it," Crosby shouted. The audience screamed. The fat woman said, "Charlie. Stop. This has gotten too crazy."

"Sweet precious angel Darleen," Crosby shouted, "you have deserved this prize for years. Betty Bruckle cheated you out of it for years by giving the prize to her sister-in-law. I put a stop to that—for you, Darleen!"

Crosby continued to back away in the direction of the rear door of the Creative Activities building. "Just keep away," he said, "and the boy won't get hurt." The door was propped open. Bright August sunlight streamed in, backlighting the murdering, crooked, back-up pie judge and his hapless victim.

Suddenly, something blocked the light coming through the door. The crowd gasped again. Thorson mouthed something to Lyle.

The audience had gone quiet. Darleen stammered. "Ch-ch-ch Charlie. S-s-s-stop! Watch out!" Crosby became confused.

Crosby swiveled around and Lyle slipped out of his grasp. "Cuddles?" Lyle said incredulously.

Crosby was face to face with a 1500-pound Black Angus bull that was supposed to be dead but wasn't. And this time, the bull was angry.

Cuddles stepped forward into the room and cornered Crosby next to the Gedney Pickle booth, pushing him over into a box of foam pickle hats. Lyle grabbed Cuddles by his halter and calmed him down.

"Cuddles!" he shouted. "You're alive!" He threw his arms around the black beast's neck.

Thorson stepped in and held Crosby until the Falcon Heights police were back on the scene. The cops cuffed Crosby and read him his rights.

"Darleen!" Crosby called out to his wife, who was covered in chocolate cream pie and sobbing over her now-ruined knock-off purse.

"Darleen, I did it all for you. I got so mad that she never let you win even though your pies tasted so bad. That shouldn't have mattered. You worked hard on them. Yes, I killed her. I got that bull to make it look like she'd been gored. I coaxed him all the way across the fairgrounds in the middle of the night and waited all night and all morning until security came. But who knew the damn bull didn't have horns?"

He began to plead. "Darleen, can you ever forgive me?"

Meanwhile, Thorson's wife approached. She too was covered in pie.

"Go home, Helen," Thorson said. "Just go home. You'll get your check."

Helen left, defeated and sticky with Darleen Crosby's extremely awful strawberry-rhubarb pie.

Thorson approached Nando. "Good aim," he said. "And good eye for detail."

"Am I off the hook, detective?" Nando asked.

"We might need you to testify, but yes, you are off the hook. Go get cleaned up for your Slovakians."

Nando grinned, and this time Thorson didn't look away.

Thorson had one more person to say goodbye to. And a bull to thank. Belatedly, an ag department student vet had turned up. He shook his head after listening to Cuddles thumping heart.

"He must have been stunned—the bullets ricocheted off his thick skull and left only a flesh wound. Other than that, he's as healthy as ever."

Lyle affectionately scratched Cuddles massive neck.

"He's gone from murder suspect to hero all in one day. He saved your life, didn't he?" Thorson said. "I guess that's what makes him a champion."

"You got that right, sir! Thanks for believing in him."

"You're very welcome, Lyle. And thank you, Cuddles!"

Unpaid Debt

"That bastard owes me fifty bucks," Juut said, and not very quietly.

"He *owed* you, you mean," Lisa told him, "For God's sake, what a thing to say at the man's burial."

Juut Nesse and his wife, Lisa, stood together near a grove of fragrant cedar trees, not far from where Chance Frazier had just been lowered into his grave. Given the oppressive heat of the summer day, the astringent perfume was even more powerful, almost otherworldly. Were he not so hell-bent on the debt owed to him by the dead man, Juut might have welcomed its reviving powers and reflected on how it was the perfect tonic for the living in a place of final repose.

"You'd think he did it on purpose," Juut said a bit quieter, but not much. "Dying before paying me back."

"Juut, you think it's all about you. Well, it's not." Lisa attempted a scolding look, but Juut wasn't having it. "Have a sense of decency, at least?"

The appeal to decency did nothing to change Juut's selfish expression.

"This is so unlike you, Juut. What happened to your generosity? It used to mean nothing to you to help somebody out."

Juut knew he'd changed. Were it not for his former and now deceased friend's actions, he might still be that considerate man. But he couldn't forgive Chance for never paying him back. That it was now too late did nothing to lessen the sting of the unpaid debt.

"There's Nona, I'm going to have a word with her," Lisa said. "Since you refused to go to the funeral, it's the first chance I've had to express my sympathy." Lisa began to walk away, but not before issuing another order. "You stay here and calm the hell down, Juut. It's over. You won't see those fifty dollars again but look at the good side. You won't see him either."

Juut watched Lisa walk toward Nona, who was standing alone at Chance's graveside. Though it had been a long time, perhaps as much as a decade since he'd seen her, he could see that Nona hadn't changed. Even in shapeless mourning black, she had a killer figure. Juut suspected that the green eyes under the dark glasses still sparkled with calculating intelligence. In some respects, he knew Nona Frazier even better than he knew his ex-friend.

For Nona was Juut's ex-wife.

Chance had borrowed far more than a few dollars from his former friend. He'd been immediately attracted to Juut's wife within days of when Juut brought her—then his fiancée—home to Los Angeles from a college in the Midwest. Chance ran off with Nona a few weeks after Juut married her and had never given her back.

Juut believed he had gotten over Chance stealing his wife—it had been twenty years since they'd eloped. And Juut had Lisa after all. They'd been married far longer than the blink of the eye that constituted Juut's marriage with Nona.

Still, the fifty dollars Chance owed him had stuck in his craw for two decades. Chance had borrowed the money the day before hitting the road with Nona, promising to repay him as soon as he could. Juut learned later that the money had been used to help pay for the quickie divorce.

He watched as Lisa approached Nona, head bowed. Lisa embraced the widow after saying a few sympathetic words, and then he thought he saw Nona say his name, her mouth pursed in a question. Lisa pointed to where he stood. In moments, both women walked to his side.

"Juut," Nona said before Juut had attempted as much as a somber nod. "I've already told Lisa I'd like to pay my husband's debt to you as soon as possible."

Juut tried to understand what was happening. "Lisa, what did you tell her just now?"

A pained expression fell across Lisa's already sad face. "What did I say to her? What do you mean?"

"—Juut," Nona broke in. "All Lisa did was express her sympathy. It was my idea to come and speak with you. In fact, I'd been hoping you'd come. I was disappointed not seeing you at the funeral. I was about to leave when Lisa walked up."

Juut was stunned by Nona's apparent pleasure in his appearance. He remembered he should say something, but it would have meant expressing sadness at Chance's passing. And he was still too annoyed to do that.

"I intend to take care of Chance's debt to you," Nona said, wiping away an unseen tear. It was hard to tell if she was crying at all, especially with the dark sunglasses covering her eyes. But she must have been, Juut thought. Her husband had just died.

Juut managed to swallow some of his pride. "Nona, really it isn't necessary, and especially not today, of all days."

"I insist," Nona said. "Consider it part of my grieving process. You'll help me with that, wouldn't you, Juut?"

"Of course he will," Lisa said for him, though to be honest, Juut wasn't sure he wanted to help Nona get over Chance. His loathing for Chance trumped his budding compassion for Nona.

Would it be enough to have Nona serving as proxy in paying off Chance's obligation? Would that release the debt that the deceased man could no longer service?

"You seem a little uncertain," Nona said. "I've seen that face before."

Juut had been wildly attracted to Nona's flair, but always hesitant about her rash behavior. Leaving the Midwest to come to Los Angeles though she knew no one, and hardly knew Juut, surprised Juut. The quick engagement had been all her idea, Juut reluctantly agreeing to the challenge in the lively green eyes.

She'd instantly fallen in love with him, she'd said, though by the time Juut had completely fallen for her, she was already flirting with Chance. Juut could almost see her bright eyes flashing under the dark glasses, but he wasn't sure whether it was anger, grief, or a flirtatious and improper invitation.

"Of course," he said at last. "Whatever you need, Nona." He'd taken the bait, hoping for the best.

"Then would you mind stopping by our... my house today? The sooner I pay you back, the better."

"Well, I..." he said "...need to bring Lisa home, but I could come over after that."

"Perfect," Nona said, clasping his hands and giving them a squeeze. "It would mean the world to me to get Chance's debt off my chest. Then I'll be able to move on. And I'll have you to thank for it!" She seemed so genuine that Juut's misgivings began to ease. Lisa and Juut watched as Nona drove off.

"Well," Lisa said at last, glancing toward the open grave. "Aren't you going to pay your respects, even once? He was your best friend, even if it was a long time ago."

Juut stepped into the blazing sun and made his way to the gaping hole where Chance's casket lay. He considered how the freak accident that had claimed Chance's life—a faulty garage door that unexpectedly closed and struck him on the head with the force of an axe—might now bring final closure to a bitter grievance. Had Chance lived, this might never have been the case.

Juut couldn't quite understand how Chance had managed to get himself killed. Garage doors had safety mechanisms that shut them off to prevent such incidents, Juut knew very well. And even though Chance was no mechanic, he should have known better than to let it fall into disrepair if that was what happened. Well, it happened and there wasn't time to sit in the stifling heat thinking about garage door failures. Nona was expecting him.

As he walked past the cedars on his way to his car, buzzing cicadas embarrassed the quiet graveyard with their incessant courting calls. Juut hurried past the noise to where an impatient Lisa waited in the sun, the reviving scent of the cedars still a mirage to his nostrils.

* * *

"Come in," Nona said to Chance from the shadow of her vestibule, "before you let the heat in." He'd hardly stepped inside the house when Nona bade him to follow her. As Juut's eyes took their time adjusting to the dim interior of Nona's home, it was hard to see where she was headed and Nona had not yet changed out of her widow's garb, so Juut had nothing to go on but the sound of her voice.

"This way." Nona's voice coiled just ahead of Juut leading him around the vestibule wall, down a narrow and curving hallway, and into another room. When Juut stepped out of her hallway and into her darkened living room, a foot shifted awkwardly, and he fell and twisted his ankle, realizing too late that the sunken living room was a half-step lower than the hallway that led to it.

"Everyone makes that mistake," Nona said, without an apology, sounding more irritated by the inconvenience of Juut's accident than his pain.

Juut heard Lisa in the back of his head. *It isn't all about you, Juut. For God's sake, have some decency.* But it was hard to be understanding of the grieving widow's pain when his ankle was smarting like a son-of-a-bitch.

"Just wait here," Nona said, "I'll give you back what Chance borrowed, then send you on your way."

Juut's eyes finally adjusted, and while he waited for the throbbing to subside, he glanced about the room and saw that it was devoid of the usual assortment of family photos, so unlike the inviting feel of his own living room. In fact, the room was completely empty except for a small table in the center of the room holding a half dozen sales flyers. They were glossy realtor brochures, describing the Frazier house. Nona had wasted no time in putting it up for sale.

He heard Nona's footsteps heading his way, and he attempted to put some weight on his sore ankle, only to feel it smart and stiffen. When Nona approached, he saw she was carrying a hammer.

"Here," she said holding it out to him, "Isn't this yours?"

The hammer was an old one, and didn't look particularly familiar to Juut. Had he lent Chance a hammer? Chance had a bad habit of borrowing things— such as one's wife—and not returning them. So, it was likely this was his hammer, but strange to think that Nona thought that returning a hammer would clear up the debt between Juut and Chance. Didn't she know about the fifty dollars?

"The bottom of the handle," Nona said. "That's your name, right?"

"Yes," Juut said, "That's my name. Chance must have borrowed it long ago." Juut took the hammer, turning it over in his hands. "Seems to have gotten stained by something?" A rusty stain had worked its way into areas of the handle and tinged the head.

"Oh," Nona said. "I guess that I didn't get all of Chance's blood off it. But it should still do what it needs, right?"

Wait. *Chance's blood?* Why would it be on a hammer? On *his* hammer?

"Oh," Juut said, the confusion suddenly erasing his ankle pain. "Was this found with him?" He pictured Chance lying on his garage floor, blood spilling from his fatal head wound to pool around a nearby hammer.

"Of course not," Nona said. "I made sure that I'd hidden it before the police and coroner arrived," she said in a business-like manner. "Don't worry, Juut," she said, obviously seeing the shock on his face. "It's been all but officially declared an accident. The case is nearly closed. And now that you have the hammer in your hands and you've put your sweaty fingerprints all over it, there's no way you would want to say it was anything else than an accident, would you?"

"You?" Juut said, incredulously. "You killed him? With this?"

Nona's green eyes glinted on his face, affirming his question without any show of remorse.

"But why? And why try to pin the blame on me?"

Nona walked to the table and collected the brochures, crumpling them into her hand. "You knew Chance. The man was always taking what wasn't his. I found that very attractive—at first—since I have a brash side myself. He took charge and just grabbed what he wanted. He never changed. There were countless affairs. Illegal finance issues at his company, expenses that showed up on other people's accounts, money that wasn't his moved into his bank account. I finally just had it."

The shock of what Nona told him hit like a hammer blow. Juut felt shaken, unstable. The ankle pain throbbed and shot up his leg. He leaned heavily against the living room wall.

"I'm not trying to pin the blame on you, Juut. Not at all. When I told you I needed help with the grieving process, I was being as honest as I could. I need your help in resolving some issues related to Chance's death. And if anything, the help I need from you will clear your name from this sordid mess. Your name is on the murder weapon, isn't it?"

"But I had nothing at all to do with this, Nona."

Another look came into her eyes, one he'd seen years ago, the night before she ran off with his best friend. She'd convincingly pretended to be in love with him to get away from her boring life in Iowa. Once she'd arrived in Los Angeles, she'd dumped him for Chance. Now she was trying to use him again to improve her life.

"And you won't, Juut, if you work with me now. You'll have a chance to completely clear your name of this, if you can help just one last time."

Juut could barely understand what was happening. He gripped the hammer in his sweaty palm, then looked at it, horrified.

"Juut. I need you to focus. Really, this will all be over soon, and I can't complete the sale of this place until the investigation is done. You see, the insurance company thought it odd that the garage door malfunctioned. They're sending someone out to inspect it. I thought maybe you would know what to do."

He knew now what she wanted.

"You'll know what to do, right?" she asked. "You're a mechanical engineer and a handyman, as I recall. You can make a few adjustments to the garage door cables. Make it look more like it could have come down on his head, just as I told them. The insurance investigator is supposed to be here in a few hours."

Juut's heart pounded. She'd been as shrewd as ever, convincing him once again that she needed him, all the while planning her escape.

"What if I were to tell them everything you've just told me," Juut said to Nona, trying to think, trying to stall. "Everything."

"Simple, Juut. I'd tell them that it's obvious you have been waiting to get back at Chance for years. That you stopped by to collect on a debt. And things went wrong. The evidence is in your hands, right now. You just stopped by after the funeral to make sure that your tracks were covered."

She'd considered everything. The bitch. There was nothing else to say. Nothing else to do but follow Nona wordlessly to the garage. Nona led him through her kitchen, out the back door, and as he followed her across the lawn, he smelled, for the first time that day, the scent of a cedar tree. There it was in Chance's back-yard, a singular tree that would have dwarfed the others in the cemetery. Without even thinking about it, Juut inhaled deeply, the sharp clean scent filling his lungs, and bringing with it a hint of salvation that could be his. By the time he exhaled, he had come up with a plan.

They arrived at the garage's service door and Nona let them inside. Chance took his time examining the garage door mechanics, the cables, and the door it-self. It was possible, he thought, and he identified just the place where a few bolts could be loosened, a wire adjusted. It just might work. Then the debt would be paid, and he'd never have a moment of worry the rest of his life.

"I'm still not sure I understand how the accident happened," he said after examining the mechanism at length. "Could you show me where you said Chance was found? I'm still not sure how I'm going to make this look convincing—as an accident, I mean."

Nona seemed more annoyed than perplexed by his request. "Really, Juut? Isn't it obvious?"

"Do you want the insurance company and the po-lice to believe you?" he asked, trying not to sound too cocky.

She sighed. "Of course." She opened the garage door, which was operating perfectly well as he expect-ed it would. She then walked to the spot where Chance had died.

"He was standing, just like that?" Juut said.

"Not exactly," Nona said. She gave him another one of her looks, and he returned a look she would have expected from him, the gullible and trusting fool he'd been to her all those years ago.

Then she turned her back to him, her conniving eyes looking away briefly. Juut gripped the hammer and brought it down hard on Nona's head. The hammer landed where he had planned, and Nona crumpled in a heap. He found a pair of gloves and quickly made the adjustments that were needed, feeling strong and sure of himself for the first time in a long time. A few moments later, he shut the door and it came down on her, creating the look of the accident she had described to perfection.

Bare Hands

A woman in her early seventies arrives at the bus stop, smiles, and notes the coldness of the weather. She compliments you on your very warm-looking coat. Her hair is softly waved, she's wearing antique pearl earrings, and her complexion is delicate and smooth despite her age. Her own coat is conservative, unflattering and modest, the kind of coat you remember your own mother wearing to church.

She immediately tells you about the mothers she's seen waiting with their children for the bus, how they have their children all bundled up, but the mothers aren't wearing any gloves. How terrible it is, all those mothers with bare hands. She shivers for them. You see her glancing at your hands, but they are buried deep in your pockets.

For once, you find yourself in a graceful conversation about nothing at all—the weather, the uncovered hands of mothers out in the cold—a small decency that one does not have to spend any time weighing for significance. What a relief it is. How you've longed for such a simple moment. For a little scene that wouldn't dream of starring in the story of your day. And it has all the flavor of a used tea bag at the bottom of your empty cup. Still, you tell yourself to enjoy it. Enjoy the moment. Isn't it what you wanted? Something completely ordinary? For once?

You shove your hands deeper in your pockets and walk away from her. The last thing you want is to engage in conversation with a stranger who will be in your life for maybe ten minutes. This, you remind yourself, is why you never take the bus anymore. It was silly to think that today's spur of the moment trip would make any difference in the life you've settled into.

You begin to ask yourself, as you knew you would, why did you bother? This little "escape" you called it, an afternoon away from work, away from the house, away from any responsibilities. You're not sure where you are going, really, you're never sure where you are going. You left the house without any real purpose. But that was the point, wasn't it? And now your hands are starting to get cold. You long to pull them out of your pockets, rub them together and blow on them, but then you'd be exposed. And you aren't sure you want, or deserve, her pity.

At last, the bus arrives, and you are surprised to hear yourself telling her, "The bus is coming." She thanks you with genuine courtesy that manages to make you cringe. You let her get on the bus before you and she drops a few quarters—the senior citizen rate—into the till. Your cold hands fumble with your dollars. You are not sure what the fare is. You manage to feed a few dollars in and make your way to a seat. She sits near the front and you find a spot a few rows back.

More passengers board every few blocks. The older woman seems to know them all, bestows on all of them that same generous smile and greeting. She chats with them about other people they apparently know in common, though for all you know, the other riders are perhaps just being polite (more polite than you were) and pretending to know what she is talking about.

The bus continues on its way, turns to follow the river bluff, and then in a few blocks, she signals and stands up. The bus stops and the bus driver asks her to wait—he'll pull ahead to a clearer spot, though she says it really isn't necessary. He does it anyway, and when she steps down, she says, "Thank you" to the bus driver. Everyone watches as she enters a small cafe where, you expect, she will greet everyone warmly inside and they will bring her the same cup of soup she orders every Monday.

Now that she's gone, you miss her. You knew you would. You almost wish you'd gotten off the bus too and gone inside the restaurant with her. You might have ordered the same soup she's having, that homey chicken vegetable soup they make that really comes from a can, but she doesn't care, it's fine with her, she wouldn't even dream of pointing out that it's the same old soup she buys from the grocery store. She will sit in her usual spot by the cashier, sipping her soup, mentioning the cold weather, telling of the mothers without gloves, cupping her hands around her coffee cup to warm them.

The bus drives on, carrying you away with your obsessive thoughts that are so desperately trying to collect themselves into a purpose you call today.

Recycle Your Dreams!

Stop holding onto your useless dreams. You may now safely dispose of them—saving money, energy, and natural resources—through the brand new Reduce, Reuse, Recycle Your Dreams Program, brought to you by the Department of Dashed Hopes (DDH).

Here's how.

Curbside recycling is now available for your unachieved dreams. Please place your tear-stained, futile imaginings in the bin labeled "dustbin of history" and leave the bin at your curb. The DDH regularly drops by to pick them up and deliver them to a dream recovery facility where they will be washed, sorted, reprocessed and implanted in some other idiot with even wilder expectations than you had.

That dream to make a difference (or a cool million) by your thirties is long past its expiration date, it's clear to everyone but you. Face the facts: you're living in your parents' basement amid their obsolete electronics, sleeping on a rock-hard futon, and spending your hours playing on your childhood Game Boy. It's time to get rid of your baggage and move on.

The DDH is here for you in that regard.

In addition to the DDH, the Dream Liberation Army (DLA) accepts your gently used, laundered delusions of grandeur. These can be bundled and dropped off at any DLA Center. The DLA is run by Gen X-ers and Millennials who foolishly went for that liberal arts major even though their parents pointed out that jobs in the petrochemical industry are far more lucrative.

Did they listen?

Oh no.

That's why they are still trying to pay off their college loans. You might consider getting a job at the DLA, even though it pays minimum wage, has part-time hours and no health care benefits except for what you can get, but still not afford, through Obamacare.

Did you know that you can also compost your abandoned hopes? Yes, you can! No matter how toxic they have been to your earnings potential and life hopes, your unattained dreams are completely organic, as you can tell by the stinking mess they have made of your life.

Making compost keeps these materials out of your daily life where they would do nothing but maintain your illusions that you still might someday be a member of the middle class.

This is clearly not happening. Get over it.

Compost those suckers by stuffing them way, way, down in your psyche and put on your red shirt and beige pants and get to work retrieving grocery carts from the Super Target parking lot. With any luck, you may wind up in management and put the rest of your generation to work as cashiers and cart retrievers. That's making a difference, isn't it?

You bet.

Bibliographical Note

Previous versions of the stories have appeared in the following places: *Ellery Queen Mystery Magazine* ("Boys will be Boys," "Tonic" and "Open Ended"); *Mystery Weekly* ("Unpaid Debt"); *Revolver* ("Playing House" and "Perpetua"); *Talking Stick* ("In the Margins," "Bare Hands" and "Everlasting Light"); *Saint Paul Almanac* ("Elephant in the Room" and "Gift Wrapped"); *Festival of Crime* ("Iced"); *Cooked to Death: Lying on a Plate* ("Whole Lotta Bull"); *Minnesota History Center* ("Stranger at the Bad Luck Ball"); *McSweeney's Internet Tendency* ("Recycle Your Dreams").

About the Author

A native Minnesotan, Susan Koefod spent much of her girlhood taking long bicycle rides and walks through hilly Dakota County and along the Mississippi River. Such excursions typically filled her imagination with poetry and story ideas. She invariably thought of herself in the third person and was the first character in her early stories. Ultimately, she relegated herself to the background as she could always invent more interesting characters to play the starring roles.

Susan Koefod is an award-winning novelist. Her Arvo Thorson mystery series debuted with *Washed Up* which was praised by Library Journal as "a smashing debut with astute observations and gorgeous prose." The series includes *Broken Down* and *Burnt Out*. Her latest novel is *Albert Park: a Memoir in Lies.* Her short stories have been published in *Ellery Queen Mystery Magazine* and other places. Susan is a winner of a Loft McKnight Artist Fellowship for Writers, a distinction of excellence and a $25,000 award open to Minnesota fine artists and writers. She lives in West St. Paul, Minnesota, with her family.

Susan Koefod